THE GODDESS ABIDES
was originally published by The John Day Company.

Books by Pearl S. Buck

A Bridge for Passing
The Angry Wife
Come, My Beloved
Command the Morning
Death in the Castle
Dragon Seed
The Exile
Fighting Angel
The Goddess Abides
God's Men
The Good Earth
Hearts Come Home and Other Stories
The Hidden Flower
Imperial Woman
Kinfolk
Letter from Peking
The Living Reed
The Long Love
Mandala
The Mother
My Several Worlds
The New Year
Pavilion of Women
Peony
Portrait of a Marriage
The Three Daughters of Madame Liang
The Time Is Noon
The Townsman
Voices in the House

Published by POCKET BOOKS

The Goddess Abides

PUBLISHED BY POCKET BOOKS NEW YORK

Pearl S. Buck

a novel

The Goddess Abides

THE GODDESS ABIDES

John Day edition published 1972

POCKET BOOK edition published December, 1973

This POCKET BOOK edition includes every word
contained in the original, higher-priced edition. It is printed
from brand-new plates made from completely reset, clear, easy-to-read
type. POCKET BOOK editions are published by POCKET BOOKS, a division
of Simon & Schuster, Inc., 630 Fifth Avenue, New York, N.Y. 10020.
Trademarks registered in the United States and other countries.

ʟ

A Muse-poet falls in love, absolutely, and his true love is for him the embodiment of the Muse. In many cases the power of absolutely falling in love soon vanishes; if only because the woman takes no trouble to preserve whatever glory she gets from the knowledge of her beauty and the power she exercises over her poet-lover. She grows embarrassed by this glory, repudiates it, and ends up either as a housewife or a tramp; he, in disillusion, turns to Apollo who, at any rate, can provide him with a livelihood and intelligent entertainment— and goes out of circulation before his middle-twenties. But the real, perpetually obsessed Muse-poet makes a distinction between the Goddess as revealed in the supreme power, glory, wisdom and love of woman, and the individual woman in whom the Goddess may take up residence for a month, a year, seven years, or even longer. The Goddess abides.

THE WHITE GODDESS
by Robert Graves

Part One

SHE HAD BEEN reading too long and by a light too dim. Now she closed the book and leaned back in her low chair. Through the glass wall of the house, where she lived alone, she gazed at the mountain. The sun was setting to the right, and its dying rays caught the snowy peak and suffused it in rose-red bloom. Below the peak the moving dots of color were the last skiers, gliding and twisting down the smooth white flanks until they were lost in the shadows of the dark forest at the mountain's base. Soon they would be tramping into the lodge, they would stand before the great fireplace, their damp garments smoking in the heat, they would drink and talk and boast of their prowess, then they would go to their rooms and bathe and dress in their informal evening clothes. They would eat gargantuan dinners and sit before the fire again and sing and talk their ski talk until, already half asleep, they went at last to their beds. In the morning they would rise to repeat the day before.

And she, here in her house alone, must now prepare her own solitary dinner, a small matter of a lamb chop and a salad and some fruit, and then after an hour or so of music, she would go to bed in the long bedroom that was half study. But first she must light the evening fire.

She lingered, however, watching the white peak glow and fade into silver, then into ash and at last into the night sky, unless by grace of moonlight it appeared again as a ghost of beauty. Tonight the moon was late. She rose and drew the curtains across the glass. She lit the logs in the huge stone chimney piece—too big, too big, Arnold had said when she drew the design of their house.

"How will you ever lift the logs?" he had inquired.

"You will lift them," she had replied with laughter and mischief.

He had not laughed. "I may not be here always," he said.

It was his first announcement. Looking back, remembering, she realized that he knew he was doomed to the death that came ten months later, a cruel death with pain eased only by the heaviest sedatives and final unconsciousness. Yet he had not spoken to her of death for nearly six months, and then by saying that he hoped she would marry again. He was too old for her he had maintained through all the years of their marriage, and she had denied it as steadfastly.

"Young men don't interest me," she told him, at first lightly and then with doggedness, until he was gone.

Yes, she had insisted upon the fireplace, and it was true that the logs were too heavy. When Sam, the hired man, a Vermonter and a neighbor, did not come on Sundays, she made a blaze of sticks that she could manage. But on every other morning he came to lay the fire which she demanded summer and winter, for this huge room without a fire could at night return to a primordial cave and she become a lost animal in its shadows. Her day ended with the dying blaze of the fire but she lit another in her bedroom. She always slept before the lesser fire died.

She rose to prepare her dinner, aware of sudden hunger, for she had forgotten to eat at noon in her absorption in her book. As usual before she set the table she turned on the stereophonic music. When she knew that Arnold must die before the year was ended, she had made the house ready to live in alone.

"Bookshelves along this north wall, please, Sam," she had ordered. "I'll need many books."

He had grumbled under his breath. "Dunno what you want so many books for—you only come here a couple of times a year."

It was true. When Arnold lived they came to Vermont for a month in the summer and when the children were not yet grown, they came for Christmas and skiing. She had given up her skis when Arnold fell ill, not wanting to leave him. She had not begun to ski again—not yet. Perhaps she never would. Meanwhile she would live in the vast old house in Philadelphia, where she had been born, an only child, and where she and Arnold had lived since her parents died.

Sam had built the shelves here in the Vermont house to her specification and she had filled them with books which she had always wanted to read and had never had time for while Arnold lived. And music, of course, she revived in her life, now solitary, not only the music of the great, but her own musical talent, dormant after years of wifehood and motherhood and the daily business of being Arnold's wife. She had opened the piano after his death and left it open always, invitation to practice and enjoy, and she found in the valley a retired German music master to give her lessons again. She had hungered, too, for languages, many languages, she wanted various tongues and so she had begun once more to study French—first French, she told herself, for her grandmother had been a Frenchwoman, and then Spanish and Italian and perhaps German. Out of the many occupations she provided for her life alone she might choose one and make it a profession, although Arnold had left her with enough money. She liked clothes and jewels, not for themselves, but as part of the woman she still wished to be. Who, she inquired

11

of herself, was that woman and what was to be her profession?

The amplitude of music swelled and soared into the high beams.

"You'll never get those beams hoisted to the roof," Arnold had said.

They were cedars cut from the forest that surrounded the house on three sides. She had ordered them to be stripped of bark and left in the weather of sun and snow and rain until they had aged to silver gray.

"I'll get them hoisted," she had insisted, and so she had done, Sam and a contractor between them fashioning a mighty lever with rope and crane.

The house was her own design and there was no room in it for children. She had married young, had borne her children young, and she had been a good mother. She had seen her children through early babyhood, childhood and adolescence, a son, a daughter, and then into somewhat too early marriages. Now she thought of them as friends, apart from herself, man and woman with their own concerns. Indeed she drew apart from them, needing to discover whether her life had meaning beyond wifehood and motherhood. She had enjoyed both functions in her somewhat reserved fashion, but there was a time for everything, and the time had come for something more.

In spite of the music, in the midst of the Andante, she heard a strong knock on the door. She turned and through the glass door she saw the figure of a man in ski garb.

"You shouldn't be there all alone," her children had said. "The whole area is changing now that the mountain is being developed. All sorts of characters—"

She left the counter, which was as much as she needed of kitchen, although Arnold had prophesied that she would soon be tired of nothing but a counter.

"You'll want to go back to your servants and the big house," he had told her.

But she was glad to be free, at least for a while, of the oppressive presence of servants and what she wanted to eat was easily made at the counter in one corner of this huge room. She peered now through the glass door. The light of the lamp over the dining table shone upon a man's face, a young face, the eyes dark and intense, the features strong. She opened the door.

"Come in," she said.

He stamped the snow from his boots and set his skis and poles against the stone outer wall of the house. Then he came in.

"Well?" she asked.

He hesitated, smiled, his hand outstretched.

"I'm Jared Barnow," he said, "and I'm not brash— only desperate."

"Yes?"

"I'm told that you have the only empty room in the township, and I have no place to lay my head! I'd no idea the area would be so crowded. I'm alone, and I thought it wouldn't be hard to find a place for a solitary man."

His accent was good, he was mannerly, but—

"It would be most inconvenient, I'm afraid," she said frankly.

He stood looking at her, waiting, his dark, intelligent eyes inquiring.

"I've never taken strangers into my house," she said. And then upon an impulse of loneliness she went on. "Put off your things and have something to eat. Then—"

"Thank you."

He took off his jacket and peeled off a rough sweater and she saw that he was slender, well above medium height but a graceful, compact figure, quick moving, his hair blond above the dark eyes.

"You'll want to wash up," she said. "That's my

husband's room there, and his bath—was, I mean. He's—not living."

He went in without reply to this, and she put two more chops in the oven and set another place at the table.

. . . "I don't get many holidays," he was saying an hour later.

If he noticed that she had changed to her dark red wool dress, sleeveless but long to her ankles and high at the neck, he gave no sign. He was eating with concentrated zeal.

"You went to prep school," she said.

He looked up. "How did you know?"

She smiled. "You don't look like a depressed person, but you've had to eat in a hurry before others got the food. That means boys."

"Might have been the army?"

"I think not. I have a son and I know."

He laughed. "You're right. Prep school. Then college. I finished that when I was twenty."

She was accustomed to taciturn young men, but he was not so much taciturn as self-absorbed. A single-minded young man, she guessed, one with a purpose. He had fine hands, she noticed, well kept without being overtended, a masculine hand, the fingers strong and the palm capable. He looked young enough to be her son—not that she wanted more sons!

"What do you do?" she inquired.

He pushed aside his empty plate. "For a living or for fun?"

"Both."

"I'm lucky," he said. "What I want to do for a living is also fun."

"And that is?"

"I don't suppose you know anything about electronics?"

"I know the word. My father was a physicist."

He woke instantly. "No! What was his name?"

14

"Mansfield. Raymond Mansfield."

"Not *the*—"

"Yes."

"I say!" He threw down his napkin. "Incredible luck! I stumble into a house and find the daughter of Raymond Mansfield!"

"But you're too young ever to have met him."

"I've studied his books. God, I wish he were alive! He'd know what I want to do."

"What?"

He looked at her shrewdly, shyly. "How do I know you'll understand?"

"I might."

"Well, I'm an engineer, a sort of a superengineer, I suppose. But I—my real work is inventing. I have things I've invented."

"What sort of things?"

"Well—" he looked at her and stopped abruptly. "They wouldn't interest you. They wouldn't interest any woman."

"I might be different."

"Yes, I suppose—"

He got up and went to the chimney piece and stood looking into its blazing cavern.

She called to him. "Would you mind putting on a log? The woodbox is there in the corner."

"That a woodbox? I thought it was a cabinet sort of thing."

"You're laughing at me. Well, I grant you, I've a mania for bigness."

He was rummaging for a log, choosing the longest, the heaviest, and he threw it into the fire. A fountain of sparks flew up. "You're not so big yourself. Who plays the piano?"

"I do."

"So do I."

He sat down and without effort played a movement from a Beethoven sonata. Halfway between table and

15

sink, her hands full of dishes, she listened and was amazed. A musician, a real one, playing as she had not heard a man play since her father died, playing with precision, elegance and depth! No one really understood music unless he was a scientist, her father had declared, and not just a scientist, either, oh, no, only the real ones, the theoreticians, whose language was mathematics. She had not understood mathematics until he had explained to her that it was the symbolic language of relationships. "And relationships," he had told her, "contain the essential meaning of life."

She set the dishes down softly and tiptoed to a chair. He played on until the last movement before the finale. Then he stopped abruptly and turned to face her. "I don't play the finale. It doesn't belong. Beethoven never knew how to stop the great music, and he just subsides or ends with a sudden bang. He had to finish somehow."

She laughed. "You're a blasphemer, but you're right. It's what I've often thought and never dared to say."

He was walking around the room restlessly and went to the window. The edge of the full moon was shining over the horizon.

"Do you live here all the year round?"

"No—just since my husband's death."

"Alone?"

"Yes."

"No children?"

"Both married and living their own lives—thank God!"

"You don't like children?"

"I love them, but any self-respecting woman likes to see her children on their own. Then she knows she's done a good job."

"You don't look—motherly."

She evaded this. "Is your own mother living?"

"No, nor my father. I don't remember them. In fact, I never knew them." He stopped by the piano and

16

repeated a few bars of the sonata, then stopped again and went over to the fire and stood gazing into the high flames leaping into the chimney. "I grew up with an uncle, an old bachelor who always seems surprised to see me in his house, however long I'm there."

"What is he?"

"Retired—ever since I can remember. Kind and confused—writes books about classical French poetry that no one publishes, but it doesn't seem to bother him. He's been awfully good to me, especially since he's never had the least idea of what I busy myself about. My mother was his sister."

He murmured this abstractedly, as though he were talking about someone else.

"Are you married?" she asked.

"No, but I think about it—now and then."

"The girl is chosen?"

"Well, she's chosen me, you might say."

She laughed again. Living alone, laughter was what she missed. "Is that what they do nowadays?"

"A good thing," he said, unsmiling. "I doubt I'll have time to choose for myself. My sort of work takes up the mind."

"And the heart—"

He looked at his watch. "I say, do you mind—may I stay? I'll get up early so as to have an early go at the mountain—if that doesn't upset you? I can make my own breakfast. Shall I put on another log?"

"No," she said, "and I get up early, too."

They parted then with nod and smile, and when she had cleared the table and washed the dishes she sat down at the piano and played softly while the fire died to ash.

. . . And then later, when she had finished her ritual of bath and brushing her long fair hair, when she was lying in the big bed in her own room, the fire blazing upon the high stone hearth, she fulfilled the end of each day, she lifted the telephone from its place and

17

dialed seven digits and she listened until she heard the gentle old voice.

"Is that you, my darling?" the voice inquired.

"It is I," she said.

"I have been waiting for you—a long evening, waiting."

"Are you alone?"

"Yes. Henry had an errand in the village. I have been rereading my essay on myth in the crowd mind. The boundary between myth and reality is very delicate. Myth is the dream, the hope, the faith, the vision of possibility which grows naturally into planning, and so possiblity is very close indeed to reality, may indeed at any moment become reality, and that is its ineffable magic, its luring charm. Do I bore you, my love? I am company only for myself, I am afraid, and yet you will never know what you supply me now—King David and his Bathsheba—I doubt they talked, you know! I imagine it was just the warmth of her young flesh against his—no talk needed. Lacking that, I talk—"

He broke into mild laughter and she laughed with him.

"You are laughing at me?" he inquired. "I don't mind, dear child—so that I make you laugh."

"I am not laughing at you," she told him. "I am thinking how glad I shall be when I get so old that I, too, can say anything I like. Have you taken your medicine today?"

"Oh, yes—Henry sees to that."

"Where are you now?"

"If you must know, you inquisitive female, I am just out of my bath, wrapped in a large towel, dripping water on the floor."

"Oh, Edwin," she protested. "You are incorrigible. Yes, you are, talking to me while you catch cold! Put on your pajamas at once and get into bed. Are you wearing your flannel ones?"

"Yes, darling. Henry put the summer ones away. He

18

put them away the first day of October as usual, and then it turned warm—Indian summer, you know—but he wouldn't get them out again, so I had to roast until snow fell. But you know all that. I hope you've forgotten tomorrow is my birthday?"

"I've forgotten how old you are, if that's what you mean!"

"Seventy-six, my dear love, and I still feel a stir in my central parts when I hear your voice."

"Edwin!"

"You reproach me?"

"Good night, good night, and I repeat—you're incorrigible!"

"God's blessing on you, sweetheart! When are you coming to see me?"

"Soon—very soon."

She put the receiver into its place again and lay back on her pillows, smiling. How could she explain to anyone the comfort of knowing that she was the center of an old philosopher's amiable heart? That was what she had missed most when Arnold died. She had ceased to be first with anyone, meaning of course, heterosexual that she was, first with any man. Though Edwin Steadley stirred no central part of her, she allowed him to love her, although of what love was compounded at such an age, she did not know. Perhaps it was only a formula, words to which he had been so long accustomed in the thirty years of happy marriage with Eloise, his wife, dead these twenty-four years, that they had become habit. How long ago could be measured in the terms of her own life, for when Eloise died she had been a girl of eighteen, teasing her mother to let her cut her long hair. She had thought of Edwin as an old man even then, although in reality he had been at the height of his career as a famous philosopher, and she had been his pupil in college.

Handsome and virile she had thought him, in spite of his age, and filled with an *élan* that she had not

19

associated with philosophy until she knew him. How much of this was due to Eloise it would be hard to guess, but a great deal, doubtless, for she had been articulate and ardent, and madly in love with him, developing, no doubt, every element of sex in him. She guessed at that, for Arnold had developed her in the same way, drawing her out of virgin shyness and leading her to her fullest womanhood, until since his death she had felt the currents of her sexuality stopped and protesting. Yet the original delicacy held. She was still to be sought and not to do the seeking.

The fire was dying here in her bedroom, too, and she fell asleep.

Jared Barnow was gone and so swiftly had the time passed that she could not believe the clock said nine o'clock in the morning. They had talked over the breakfast table until suddenly the clock in the corner had chimed the hour and he had leaped to his feet.

"My God, I came to ski! You make me forget. Here, I'll help with the dishes."

"No, no——"

"But, of course——"

In the end she had persuaded him and had seen him off, and then had remembered and had called him. "Come back if you don't find something nearer to the slopes!"

"Thanks!" he had shouted.

She watched him tramp down the hill to the valley road which in turn would lead him up to the ski area on the mountain opposite her window. When he was out of sight in the intervening forest, she turned to the room again. It was strangely empty, a room too huge, as Arnold had always told her.

"It's a room to get lost in," he had said one evening when the fire was casting shadows in the distant corners, and suddenly now although the sun was shining through the windows, she felt lost.

She finished the dishes, and then went into the room that had been Arnold's but now was her guest room. The bed was neatly made, and everything in order. Then he must have planned to come back again? Otherwise he would have left the bed unmade. Or if he had made the bed he would have put aside the sheets. Why did she keep thinking about him? She would call Edwin and tell him about the guest and so free herself, perhaps. This much she had learned about being alone, that she could mull over something and worry herself with it until she did nothing else.

"Although I shouldn't use Edwin merely to ease myself," she murmured, and went to the telephone and took off the receiver and dialed. Ten o'clock? He would be at his desk, writing his memoirs, the history of a long and distinguished life, spent among famous men of letters and learning.

She heard his voice on the telephone at her ear. "Yes? Who is it?"

"It's I."

"Oh, my darling—how wonderful to hear from you at the beginning of day!"

"I shouldn't be interrupting your work but I need to hear your voice. The house seems empty."

"It makes me happy that you need me."

No, it is not fair of me, she thought, to use him because I miss someone else, and besides it is impossible that I miss someone I met only yesterday and that someone a man young enough to be my son. It is only that I cannot accustom myself to living alone—not yet.

"When are you coming to see me?" the voice inquired over the telephone.

It had been agreed long ago, without words, that when they met it was she who must go to him. The hazards of traveling were too much for him now, but beyond that fact was her own inclination to keep this house jealously for herself. Even her children she did not welcome here, preferring to put them up in the guest house nearby. This house was hers, inviolate now that Arnold was gone. There were times which she would not acknowledge that even he had sometimes been an intruder. But she had never known herself as she really was until now when she was alone.

Before her widowhood she had been a daughter and sister, wife and mother, dividing herself perforce, though willingly, for she had enjoyed each relationship and treasured her memories. Now she was living with herself and by herself as though she were a stranger, discovering new likes and dislikes, new abilities. Books, for example—she had thought of books as diversion and amusement. Now she knew they were communication between minds, her own and others, living and dead. Such communication was the source of learning and she had a thirst for learning, reviving after the busy years of her married life.

"I have a guest," she said now.

"Who is it?"

She heard an echo of jealousy in Edwin's voice, and was amused.

"You're jealous!"

"Of course I am!"

"But that's absurd."

"No, only natural. I'm in love with you."

"That's nonsense."

"No, only reality. Let me tell you an amazing truth about the human being. You're too young to know, but I know. The ability to love is the secret of life. So long as one can love, really love, another human being, death waits afar off. It is only when the capacity to love ceases to exist that death follows soon. I thank you, my darling, for letting me love you. It keeps death from my door."

She listened as she always listened to him, accepting and believing. He was still teacher and she was still

22

pupil. "You make too much of me," she said, "and that is very sweet."

"So," he continued, "who is your guest?"

She told him briefly, almost indifferently, ending with the words, "And probably he won't be back. The weekend rush is over today and he'll find another place to stay."

"I hope so," he replied. "I don't like your being alone in the house with a stranger. One never knows, these days—and you're a very beautiful woman."

Arnold had not been one to praise her looks and she had never been sure of her own beauty. He had been jealous, yes, but without cause, and since he was possessive it occurred to her now that perhaps she had always been beautiful, and he had not dared to tell her so.

"It's only what you think, Edwin," she said, "but still I like to hear it, being in my secret heart a vain woman."

"You've never thought of yourself. I've always known you were beautiful. I remember the first time I saw you. It was a September day, and your head, true red gold, was shining there among the browns and blacks and blondes of the freshmen. I marked you then, without any thought of course that one day you would become my life. I saw your eyes, clear with intelligence. That's my prize pupil, I thought—as you were. And I began then to scheme how I could keep you in my department, and failed because that rascal, Arnold Chardman, married you too early! I almost wept the day you came to tell me. Remember?"

She did remember. It was true she had married too young, but she had been so joyful that she had not noticed the professor's eyes, only his silence.

"Will you not wish me well?" she had asked.

She remembered the long pause before he answered. "I wish you to be happy. You will find your happiness in different ways. Just now you are sure it is in marriage. Well, perhaps so. But the time will come when it will be in something else."

"So long as it is not in someone else," she had said gaily.

"Do not limit happiness," he had said gravely. "One takes it where one finds it."

They had not met again for years and she forgot him. Then one day, soon after Arnold had died, among the many letters of condolence she found his letter. He wrote as though they had parted only yesterday.

"Do you remember," he had written, "do you remember what I said about happiness? One happiness has passed, but hold yourself ready for the next, whatever it is. If you do not see it on the horizon, then you must create it where you are. So long as you live you may find happiness if you search for it, or create it for yourself. Perhaps the search itself is happiness."

It had been a long letter, speaking only of herself and the future, of life and not of death. Yet he, too, had known death, he reminded her, for Eloise, his wife, had died many years before. Now he lived alone in their house in the country, which had been their summer home, and he was writing books.

She had replied with a sad short letter, merely saying that his had been the most comforting words she had received, "but there is no happiness on the horizon," she had told him, "and I find no creative spark within me."

Then he had sent her a telegram, inviting her to visit him, and she had gone, only to find him the center of a houseful of grown children and grandchildren, temporary visitors, and among whom she had sat as a guest, vaguely welcome, but of no importance. It was he who had made her important, singling her out as his companion, to remain at his side when the others went off on jaunts together. Alone in the vast sprawling family house, he had talked and she had listened. He was writing a book on immortality, and he talked of what he wrote. She had listened with concentrated interest, for Arnold had not believed in life beyond death. In the midst of her anguish as he lay dying, she had admired his firm courage.

"I am very near the end," he had told her. "And it is the end, my dear. There remains only my gratitude—to you. For your infinite variety—my thanks!"

Those were his last coherent words, for he had been overcome with pain, and in a daze of agony had died a few hours later. On her first night alone in the great house in Philadelphia which was now hers only, she had pondered his words. Was it true, could it be true, that nothing of him remained except the body buried in the churchyard where his ancestors lay? She had puzzled her way among such thoughts, unable to reach conclusion, equally unwilling to believe he was right, and yet compelled to fear that he was. She had no proof of immortality, but then he had had no proof against it, either. In this frame of mind she had been willing, and indeed eager, to hear what Edwin had to say.

"We human beings are the only creatures who are able to think of our own end, without doubt or faith."

He had made this as a statement one day on her first visit. They sat on the terrace overlooking the distant mountains, and the housekeeper had brought them tea and small cakes and, setting the tray on the table between them, had gone away again. Alone with him, she had dared to disagree with him. Over her teacup she had shaken her head.

"You disagree?" he had asked, surprised.

"Even animals know their end and fear it," she had replied. "See how wildly they try to escape death! They may not be able to reason or think, but they fight death. Have you ever seen a rabbit in the clutch of a dog's jaws? Until its last breath it struggles against death. A fish, drawn out of water, will struggle to live. Animals fear death and if they fear, they know."

He had listened, surprised and pleased. "Good thinking," he had replied, "but don't confuse instinct with consciousness."

She had pondered this and then had inquired, "What is the difference between animal and human being?"

"Consciousness of self," he had said. "A human being declares himself because he knows his own being. Animals? No. They don't separate themselves from the cosmos."

They had come strangely close even on that first visit and, as time passed, had grown into mutual dependence each upon the other, although she recognized that what she felt for him was not love, only closeness. On his part it was frankly love, an old man's love, the nature of which was not close to her. Whatever it was, love was sweet, and she clung to its persistence. He was wiser than she, and this, too, was sweet. She had never leaned on anyone, for Arnold, she had discerned early, would never be able to know her altogether. They were compatible, but she was the knowing one.

Edwin's voice recalled her. "Are you still there, Edith?"

"Yes, oh, yes," she replied quickly.

"Then you haven't been listening!"

"Not quite," she confessed.

"You've been dreaming!"

"Only thinking—about you and me."

"Ah, then, I forgive you. And thank you! It's not good for me to suffer jealousy, you know—at my age."

"You needn't. Now go back to your work, dear."

She put up the receiver, turned to face the day, a bright sunlit day, the white slopes gay with darting figures, and she wasted it wantonly. A multitude of small tasks waited, a silver bowl to be polished and

26

filled with fruit, a trip to the village store which she postponed so that she could sit by the window and gaze again at the mountainside, imagining which of the flying dots of color could be that of Jared Barnow. She had never known anyone named Jared and the strange name added to his attraction. Something new, someone new, had entered her house last night.

. . . When the sun had set and shadows crept over the mountain, leaving only the peak rose-red against the sky, she busied herself with the evening meal. For two? Or only herself? She would not set the table until she knew. Meanwhile she would prepare enough food— two small steaks, the larger one for him. Then suddenly she heard his footsteps, stamping off the snow, and he opened the door without knocking.

"I'm back," he said.

"I was expecting you."

She went toward him as she spoke and to her surprise and somewhat to her horror, she felt an impulse to put her arms about him. She restrained herself. To what absurdities could loneliness reduce her! She must be on guard. A new experience, this impulse, for until now she had only to be on guard against others, her own fastidiousness—coldness, Arnold had sometimes called it, when he was angry with her—until now had been her weapon. In her own being she had known she was not cold, withdrawn perhaps into a space which she had never shared with anyone, an inner space.

"I'm back, as you see," he repeated.

"No luck in finding a room?"

"I didn't try," he said, unlacing his boots.

"I'm rather glad," she said. "It makes me feel a part of life on the mountain."

"You've never skied?"

"Oh, yes, I loved it when I was young."

"It's not too late, you know."

"I'm afraid it is."

"Nonsense! You look—about twenty-five, say!"

27

She laughed. "Add ten years and then another seven. I'm forty-two!"

"No!"

"Yes!"

"Never mention it again," he commanded. He rose and went toward the door to the guest room. "I'll just wash up a bit, brush my hair—"

"Everything is ready," she said.

He paused. "You expected me?"

"I hoped."

They exchanged a look and he went into the room and closed the door. And she stood, uncertain. Should she change her dark green wool suit? But if she did, would he suspect her of some absurd coquetry? She decided not to change and was glad, half an hour later, for he sat down and began eating with self-assurance and in a silence that was almost ingratitude, she thought. He was only young, she decided, watching him—young and very hungry. It would be absurd to change into her long red dress—or the black one trimmed in silver, merely for this greedy boy.

"How long are you staying on the mountain?" she asked at last, to break the silence. No, she was ready for him to leave, her pride wounded, remembering the foolish impulse she had resisted.

"I must go back tomorrow," he said. "I have a job in a laboratory. Well, it's more than that. It's an opportunity—a chance at last to invent, to discover—do something on my own, perhaps—Brinstead Electronics."

"A fine firm," she said.

"You know it?"

"My father was a sort of consultant."

"I wish I'd known him!"

"He died long before you were old enough to know him."

The words stung her heart with a sudden wounding of her selfhood. When he had been born she was already out of childhood, a girl quarreling with her

28

patient mother over the length—or shortness—of skirts and defending her right to come home after midnight when she was out with Arnold.

"The whole world knew him," he was saying.

"I suppose so."

Why was it difficult to talk? She felt depressed and apart, almost hostile to him because he was so young. Yet last night the conversation had flowed between them, easily and with understanding. She lifted her head involuntarily and realized that she had done so because he was staring at her, his eyes very dark under his brows. When their eyes met he spoke abruptly.

"I like you. Not just because you're beautiful, either. I'm used to that sort of thing. The girl I'm going with is pretty enough. But you have something—"

He broke off and she made herself laugh.

"Age—that's all!"

He did not reply with laughter. Instead he spoke almost with irritation. "I wish you wouldn't talk about age! I'm ashamed of being—foolishly young. I've always been too young for what I wanted to do—too young to go to college, too young for a job. I ran away when I was fifteen, just to pass the time until I was older. I finished college too young. I've always done everything too young."

"Where did you run?"

"I traveled—loafed would be better—around the world for two years."

"So now you're—"

"Twenty-four."

She stabbed herself again. "Tell me about your girl."

He frowned and turned his head toward the window. Over the rim of the mountain a slim new moon hung suspended, a decoration in the sky.

"She's not my girl exactly," he replied, still irritably.

"Why not?"

He pushed his plate aside, rose and went to the window. There he stood gazing at the shadowed mountain and the hanging moon.

"I'm in a strange situation," he said.

"Yes?" Her voice invited.

"I'm always too young for what I want to do, but I'm too old for—for girls."

A moment of silence hung between them, as tenuous, as quivering, as the new moon, glimmering in the clouds now drifting above the mountain.

"I don't quite know what you mean," she said at last, her voice gentle.

"I don't, either," he said abruptly and came back to the table and sat down. "More coffee, please. What's your name, by the way? Your first name—"

"Edith."

"Edith," he repeated. "Edith? I never knew anyone with that name. My mother had a silly name—Ariadne. Still, it's rather sweet. As I said, I don't remember her, but my uncle said she was a sweet person."

"What happened to them?" she asked in the same gentle voice.

"They were killed in a motor accident when I was two. Yet I seem to remember someone like my mother, a soft pretty someone—but probably I don't remember, really—just a dream, perhaps, or even pure imagination."

"And there's been no one to take her place?"

"No. My uncle never married. Didn't I tell you? I suppose he has a mistress tucked away somewhere. We never discuss such matters."

"No one has ever taken your mother's place?"

"I've never looked for anyone. Mothers are irreplaceable, aren't they?"

"Yes," she said firmly, and then after a moment, "but the girl? Is she younger than you really?"

"Not so many years—but otherwise—" He shrugged slightly. "Yet she's clever enough, intelligent, all that. But I'm too old for her. I'm too old for myself. I'm a burden even to myself."

She laughed. "Oh, come now!"

He did not reply with laughter. "Yes, I am that. I'm interested in too many things, not people. So much I want to do! I've no time for—for marriage and so forth, and that's what this girl wants."

"Is she in love with you?"

"She says so."

"And you?"

"I? When I'm with her, I'm normal enough to feel the stir, you know! But the old part of me knows better. 'You'll be bored with her.' That's what it tells me—am I mad?"

"No. Only wise."

"I could do with less wisdom."

"Don't say that. It's given to you as a tool for accomplishment."

"Of what?"

"Of whatever it is that you want to accomplish."

"To penetrate the secrets of the universe!"

He leaned forward, elbows on the table, his eyes shining into hers, and she felt comforted, even elated, for some vague reason she did not wish to comprehend.

"I must leave early tomorrow morning," he said abruptly, and as abruptly went to the piano and began to play.

Snow fell upon snow, in silence and chill. It began as he left the house the next morning, the sky gray and the mountain clouded in mist. Winter settled over the eastern coast. In Philadelphia, too, it was snowing, her radio had announced.

"I hate to leave this warm house," he said.

31

He stood at the door, wrapped in his rough outdoor coat, its cap falling back.

"You are leaving your skis in the cellar. That means you will be back," she said.

"Yes, but I mean this morning."

"This morning," she echoed.

She could not tell him what she was thinking, what she always thought when snow was falling. Arnold, lying under the snow! Of course she was accustomed by now, if she was ever to be accustomed, that is, and why should it be the snow? In the spring she could contemplate his grave without agony, and in the autumn the bright leaves falling from a maple tree near his grave made the city churchyard almost cheerful. But the snow? The realization of his death, desolate and final, had come at the first snowfall and she was alone here in this house. She had stood at the wide window, biting the knuckles of her clenched right hand, tears streaming down her cheeks. O Arnold, you lying alone under the snow!

Something of that desolation fell upon her now. The house had been full today of this presence, young and strange, yet he was no longer a stranger to her, nor ever had been or could be. Something they shared, something more than music, but what? He had been very gay this morning, almost as though he were glad to go, until at this moment when he stood tall above her, and she saw a look in his eyes, startled and unbelieving.

"Yes, I like you," he said and so suddenly, as though he had made a discovery, that she laughed.

"Delightful to hear," she said gaily, "and of course you'll come back. The only question is when."

"I'll let you know." He stood looking at her and then abruptly he turned and left her, closing the door firmly behind him. She lingered for an instant, gazing at that closed door. The house was silent about her, and empty.

. . . "The sunsets are always finest when you are here," Edwin said.

She was sitting by the small round table in the bay window of his great square living room. In the distance mountain ranges lifted sharp peaks against a glowing western sky. It was her usual place when she was in this vast old house in the evening, and she seldom missed the sunset when the sky was clear. Today, the second day of her visit, had been very clear. She had spent the hours with "your old philosopher" as he called himself until, an hour ago, he was overcome with one of his fits of weariness and had gone upstairs to sleep. Now he had waked and had come to find her.

"The sunset is always finest after snow," she replied.

She felt his hands on her shoulders, his cheek gently pressing her hair.

"The unutterable comfort of you, of having you in my house," he murmured.

"I am always happy here," she replied, motionless, her gaze upon the sky.

The colors were changing now, the violence of crimson and gold subdued to rose and pale yellow.

33

"Don't move," he said as she was about to rise. "I have something to ask of you."

"Yes, Edwin?"

He was standing behind her and thus out of her sight, his hands still on her shoulders. In the silence she turned her head and saw an unusual tenderness suffusing his face as he looked down into her eyes.

"Is it something outrageous?" she asked, smiling.

"I am wondering if you will so consider it. But no—you will understand. I think so. In your own way you are an artist, with an artist's honesty."

"Perhaps you had better prepare me."

He came from behind her then and sat down opposite her at the small table. His head, the white hair and clipped white mustache, the fair, healthy skin and bright blue eyes, made him a handsome portrait against the fading sky.

"How you can look as you do!" she exclaimed.

"How do I look?" he demanded.

"I shan't tell you. You're vain enough already."

"That is to say—I'm lovable? For you, I mean?"

"Of course. You know that. Every time you ask me I tell you so."

"Ah, but I have to ask," he complained.

"So that I have courage to confess!"

They were bantering on the edge of truth again and beyond it they had never ventured. Or perhaps she was not ready for truth, and perhaps would never be. What she felt for him was an emotion altogether different from the willing love she had given Arnold. But that love had ended, stopped by death, and suddenly, for a while, there was no one to love. In the long months when she knew he must die she had wondered about love. Would it go on living after the beloved was dead? Could so strong a force continue to feed only upon memory? She knew now that it could not. The habit of love became a necessity to love and remained alive in her being, like a river dammed. Now it was flowing

34

again, not in fullness, not inevitably, but tentatively and gently toward this man who sat facing her, his back to the sunset. He began to speak in his thoughtful, philosophizing mood, his eyes, so piercing in their blue, upon her face.

"The need to love and be loved lasts until we draw our final breath and from the need comes the power. It is in you, it is in me. How can this be, you may ask. Because, my child, my dear and only One, love sustains the spirit and the spirit sustains life. If love is mutual, then the two concerned can live long. Yet even if it is one-sided, the one who loves is sustained. It is sweet to be loved, but to be able to love is to possess the life force. I love you. Therefore I am strong. Whatever my age, I am sustained by my own power to love. How fortunate am I to have someone I can love! For I am fastidious, my darling! It is not every woman who is to be loved—at least by me."

She felt an embarrassment entirely new to her, for at this instant there was something new about him. Whether it was the light of the sky beyond him, or a light shining from within him, he was for the moment transfigured, his face younger by years, his eyes bright, a faint flush on his cheeks. He leaned toward her impulsively.

"Let us have no reserves! I want you wholly. I want to give myself wholly."

"What do you mean, Edwin?" she asked.

She was imprisoned by his gaze into her eyes, by his hands seizing upon hers with unexpected strength.

"May I come to your room tonight?" he asked abruptly, as though he struck down a barrier with one blow.

The question hung between them, unbelievable, yet an entity. He had spoken. There could be no doubt that he had spoken, and question demanded answer. She was compelled by his unchanging gaze. In her silence he spoke again, this time gently, as to a child.

"We inhabit these bodies, my darling. They are our only means of conveying love. We speak, of course, but words are only words. We kiss, yes, but a kiss is only a touch of the lips. There is the whole body through which the sacred message can be exchanged. And for what do we nurture the body with food and drink and sleep and exercise except for the conveyance of love?"

When she hesitated, transfixed by sudden shyness, he laughed, but gently.

"Don't be afraid, my child! I have been quite impotent these ten years. I wish only to lie quietly at your side in the darkness of the night, and know that finally we are one, never again to be separate, however far apart we may be."

She was able to speak at last. She heard herself say words as unbelievable as those he had spoken. Yet she spoke them.

"Why not?" she said. "Why not?"

. . . They parted as usual after the usual late dinner. In the presence of Henry the butler they said good night formally and so wholly as usual that she half wondered whether she had not imagined the sunset scene. And knew she had not, for with an instinct, long dead, now in her own room she searched among her garments until she found a lace-trimmed nightgown. She wore plain suits by day, their simplicity becoming her classic face, but secretly, at night, ever since she had been alone, she bought and wore, now that Arnold was dead, those fragile exquisite confections that he had disliked. Pajamas suited her better, he had said, and so she had worn them until he was gone. Then, and who could possibly understand this, the very day after his funeral she had gone to the finest shop in the city, and had bought a dozen nightgowns, wisps of lace and silk and, quite alone, she decked herself nightly for sleep.

Thus she decked herself now, after her scented bath,

and standing before the mirror she brushed her long fair hair and braided it as usual and climbed into the high old bed as though nothing were about to happen, and lay there, her heart beating in expectant alarm that was also reluctantly pleasurable. Should she sleep— could she sleep? Debating it, she fell into a light slumber without being aware that she did so. She was wakened by his voice. He was bending over her, a lit candle in his hand.

"I knocked, you know, darling, but there was no answer. And so I came in, hoping to see you beautiful in sleep as I have been doing these last five minutes. Now I know what sleep does to your dear face. You were almost smiling."

He put the candlestick on the bedside table, he lay down beside her as though it were already habit and, slipping his right arm beneath her head, he lifted her to his shoulder.

"Now then, we're comfortable, aren't we? And we are as we should be, man and woman lying side by side in mutual trust. I shan't ask you to marry me, my love. It wouldn't be fair to you. I'm too old."

"What if I ask you?" she inquired. Comfort, sweet and profound, flowed into her blood.

"Ah, that would be a question," he replied.

But no, she thought, she would never ask it. Marriage? She had no wish for it. Marriage would make her think of Arnold. Let her explore this relationship with Edwin quite free of memories!

Suddenly he threw back the covers and sat up to survey her. "What's this lovely thing you have on, this gossamer garment, this silver cobweb?"

She lay smiling in enjoyment of his pleasure. "You like it?"

"Very much, but—"

He broke off and she felt his hands dexterously slipping the lace from her shoulders, from her breasts,

37

her waist and thighs, until the garment that had covered her lay in a soft heap at her feet.

"Blessed be our bodies, for they are the means of love!" he whispered.

She did not reply, choosing to allow him to lead where he would, watchful only for distaste in herself. But there was no distaste. Nothing she had ever known prepared her now for his grace, his delicacy, the sureness of his touch. The philosophy of love! The phrase sprang into her mind. This was more than physical, whatever it was. Then he put aside the robe he wore and lay beside her again.

"Now we know each other," he said. "We can never be strange to each other from this hour on."

There in the night they lay in each other's arms, passionate and passionless. The moon rose high and shone through the wide window and she saw his body, beautiful even in age, the shoulders straight, the chest smooth, the legs slender and strong. He had given his body respectful care, and was rewarded even now. And how many women had loved this body? Impossible that so powerful a beauty of mind and body had not combined often in the act of love! But she felt no jealousy. This was her hour, her night. And it was true that, knowing themselves as they were, they could never again be far apart.

"Yes," she said clearly and aloud.

"Yes, what, my sweet?"

"Yes, I love you."

He gave a long sigh and drew her against him. "I thank God," he said. "Whom I have not seen, I thank. Once more, before the end, to love and be loved! What more can I ask!"

With this he fell into light sleep. But she lay awake, still in his arms, awake and thinking of the strangeness, that she lay in Edwin's arms, in this room, in his house. She was not in the least regretful. What he had said was true, it was right, but strange, nevertheless. And suddenly she forgot where she was, and fell to thinking instead of Jared Barnow. Would he ever come back again? And why should he come again, and indeed she did not care now whether he did or did not. In the moonlight Edwin's profile was marble white, pure and perfect. She felt new reverence for the beauty of this body and the splendor of this mind. It was honorable to be chosen for love by this man, this famous man, visited even now by great men and women from everywhere in the world. And if her quiet love could add a day to his life, words to his thoughts, strength to his frame, was not this, too, a sort of joy?

. . . She returned to her mountain house the next day and waited for the weekend. Snow fell and continued to fall day and night until on the north side of the house it drifted almost to the eaves. Sam, bringing logs, tunneled his way into the back door.

"How can people come for the weekend even to ski?" she demanded.

He grinned. "They'll come because the roads 'ull be open. Folks here know that snow is their bread and butter."

Reassured, she waited for the weekend. Then he would come. Jared Barnow—she spoke his name to herself and was shocked. How could she think of him after what had happened with Edwin? She searched her heart, her mind, to discover memories, not so much of guilt as of distaste. There were none. Could it be possible that she sought further completion of some sort? Of what sort? And what had Edwin to do with Jared? And why ask questions, especially when she wished no answers? Let life lead her where it would! She felt herself floating, passive, waiting for whom, for what, she did not know, she would not ask.

. . . "I don't see you here in this house, you know," Jared said.

He had come on Friday night, exactly as though she

expected him, which she did and did not, hoping that he would come and again that he would not.

"You'll have to be careful for the first year or so," Amelia had said—Amelia, her old childhood friend, whose house was in Philadelphia next door to her own childhood home and who was still there, unmarried and living alone in a houseful of inherited servants. It was less than a week after Arnold died, and she had not been able even to speak his name aloud, but Amelia was without tact and said whatever she liked and at all times. They were in the upstairs sitting room, where she and Amelia had cut out paper dolls, had accumulated records, had designed frocks, had met for a last moment before her wedding and now were meeting after Arnold's death.

"What do you mean, Amelia?" she had asked.

Amelia had shrugged her shoulders. "I'm not speaking from experience, of course, but I've heard Mamma say that after Papa died—I was only three—she was so lonely that she was tempted to marry any man that asked her. After she got over that year she knew she didn't want to marry at all."

"I shan't want to marry again, either," she had murmured. Much as she relied on Amelia for diversion, she had never been able to confide everything to her, especially as Amelia, being rather plain and certainly too blunt, had never been in love, so far as she knew. The crudity of Amelia's remarks had stayed in her memory, however, and she recalled them now as she replied to Jared.

"How do you see me?" she asked.

"In a great beautiful house somewhere," he replied promptly, as though he had thought about it. "I see you with servants to wait on you. I hate you to be here alone. I don't want you to cook my breakfast. I make my own bed for I can't bear to think of your doing it. Only when you're at the piano there, or sitting on that high hearth in the firelight, do I feel I'm really seeing you."

She was moved by his earnestness. "Thank you," she said. "And you don't know how you help me. I've known I must go back to the big house but I haven't had the courage. I came away after my husband's death, and I've lingered on, dreading to go back alone—"

He interrupted her. "I'll be with you. What I mean is—I'll come to see you immediately and stay over a weekend, at least, now and then, if you'll let me."

"Of course," she said. "I'm very touched, and you mustn't for any reason, think it necessary. I shall be quite all right once I'm there—in a day or two. I have friends next door. My husband and I grew up in that neighborhood. In fact, it was a question whether we'd live in his family home or mine. But my house was empty—my father died soon after my marriage and my mother died earlier. I was an only child and so everything was left to me, and I'm really fond of the house."

She spoke breathlessly, trying to explain all at once and not knowing quite what it was she wanted to explain. He listened raptly until she broke off.

"Perfect," he said. "That's where I want to see you, in a house that is your setting. This?" His arm swept the rugged room. "No!"

And then as though he had settled an argument he went abruptly to the piano and began to play a resounding polonaise of Chopin's creation, and she sank into the deep sofa before the fire and listened, entranced by his new interpretation of familiar music. By his emphasis he eliminated every hint of the pathos that underlay the music and made instead a triumphant assertion of life.

"And what would Chopin have thought of that?" she inquired when he had finished as abruptly as he had

41

begun and rising had come to stand over her, his brooding eyes upon her face.

"I make all music my own," he replied, not removing his gaze.

And she kept smiling, half shy, half afraid. She did not know him. He was still a stranger. All the more dangerous then was this powerful attraction which had no basis in knowledge. She would have liked to ask him what his thoughts were and dared not. He spoke them without her asking.

"I want you to come skiing with me tomorrow."

Her reply was instant. "I couldn't possibly!"

"Why not?"

"Well, for one thing, I have no skis."

"We can rent them."

"I haven't skied for years."

"That's an argument for—and this is probably the last good snow of the year."

"It's not good snow. Sam says the slopes are icy—warm sun melts them by day and freezes them by night."

"It might snow tonight. There are clouds on the mountaintop."

"And a shining moon!"

"Let's finish this argument in the morning."

"The answer will be the same."

"Not if snow falls in the night—no, don't speak! I shan't let you."

He put his hand over her mouth and held it there until, choking with laughter, she pulled it away.

"God, what a soft mouth you have!" he exclaimed, wondering.

"I'd have bitten your hand if it weren't so hard," she retorted. "And I don't want to ski."

"Stop there," he cried, "or I'll do it again. I won't take no for answer."

"You shan't have yes, at any rate," she retorted.

"For tonight, then, let it be neither yes nor no."

She rose, half afraid. He looked at her steadily, speculating, but on what? She stepped back, he shook his head.

"I don't believe it," he said.

"What?" she asked.

"Your age."

"You must believe it."

He shook his head again and then suddenly he reached for her hand, took it, turned it over and kissed the palm. "I'll never believe it."

She stood, unresisting, astonished, the kiss in her hand an unexpected gift. He let her hand fall gently to her side.

"Good night," he said abruptly and crossed the room to the door of his room. There he paused.

"I shall pray for snow," he said and closed the door.

. . . In the night the snow fell. She woke after a few hours of restless sleep and rose from her bed and drew aside the gold-colored draperies of the glass doors facing the mountain. The light of her bedside lamp was reflected upon a curtain of soft white flakes thickly falling. The terrace outside was already newly covered. She would never be able to resist his determination now, and already yielding she returned to her bed and slept.

"My prayers are always answered," he declared in the morning at the breakfast table.

"But I still have no ski clothes," she said.

"All the more fun! We'll outfit you at the ski shop, and get on our way. Come on, hurry up, no loitering over coffee, if you please! The sun is climbing fast. A good six inches of snow, though——"

"You're really rather domineering!"

"It's my nature," he agreed cheerfully.

He got up as he spoke, gathering dishes, began washing and drying and putting away while she watched, amused, and finished her coffee.

"You're very expert," she said.

"I've camped all over the world. Last year I was in the Himalayas."

"Doing what?"

"Studying cosmic rays. Ever hear of a fellow called Tesla?"

"Of course. He wanted to electrify the globe, didn't he, and provide an eternal source of electric power?"

"God, you're knowledgeable!"

"I'm my father's daughter. He believed that Nikola Tesla was infinitely greater as a scientist than Edison was. In fact, he wrote articles about Tesla—and introduced him to millionaire benefactors sometimes."

"We'll have to talk about Tesla tonight, before the fire. Now the mountain waits."

He hustled her ruthlessly, he was impatient and unrelenting, and in half an hour they were in the ski shop, he ordering expertly and refusing argument against the latest in ski clothes, garments of which she had not heard in the years that had passed since she taught the children to ski.

"Skin tight," he ordered. "That's for fair weather like today. You feel as though you had nothing on. Fits you like your own skin."

He studied her critically when she came out of the dressing room in the tight suit that covered her from neck to ankles. He gathered an inch of slack at her waist.

"You can take a smaller size," he said. "You've the waist of a girl."

He sent her back, and she slid into another suit, and came out again for inspection.

"Perfect," he declared. "Now for warm-up clothes. No more long underwear these days! You slip on a sort of space suit overtop. . . . And the skis—they're new, too—plastic core and fiberglass—fine for any kind of snow, ice, crud, moguls, powder. Boots, please, young woman"—this to the bewildered clerk. "Leather on the

44

outside, foam inside, and single buckles, though in my opinion the perfect boot is still to be made. Maybe I'll think of something someday."

She was ready at last and they climbed into their seats in the lift. The snow had ceased but the sky was leaden gray again and ready to let fall, but perhaps not until evening. All through the day they skied and she was childishly proud that her old skills were with her still. He praised her but he was critical.

"Your timing is not quite—look, you have to do three things at once, see? Pole plant, upweighting, switch your leading ski, like this! But keep your skis on the snow—very slight upweighting!"

He illustrated in a series of skillful turns and she saw that he was superb on skis, even as he was at the piano. He continued to teach her throughout the day, and she strove to perfect herself, her good body responding to new demands.

"Your traverse," he was saying, "it's a little awkward. Don't pay heed to your shoulders. It's your hip you must watch—hold the downhill hip back and everything else—body, shoulders, everything—will be ready for the traverse."

She practiced again and again and not until sunset did she realize her exhaustion and even then it was he who recognized it first.

"I've worn you out and damn me for a perfectionist! You ski beautifully and what I've been insisting on are just the final touches."

She protested. "But I'm a perfectionist, too, and I love it!"

He flung his arm about her shoulders. "Good companion! Let's go home and dine in front of a roaring fire."

Which they did, he grilling the steaks before the fire while she tossed salad in the great salad bowl of Burmese teak.

They ate in silence, and afterward he turned on

45

stereophonic music and they listened in silence but sleep overcame them.

"I must go to bed," she murmured, her eyes half closed.

"So must I," he confessed.

They rose, they stood hesitating, and for a drowsy moment she thought, she imagined, he was about to kiss her. Instead he straightened and stepped back.

"Good night, sweet friend," he said.

To which she answered nothing and indeed could not, for all her strength was needed for her own control. She would not, she would not invite the kiss, for to what end it might lead she could not foretell and dared not ask.

"Good night," she said, and stumbled, still half in sleep, across the room to her own door.

In the night she woke to the patter of rain upon the roof. That was the end of snow, then, and of skiing. Tomorrow he would be gone and she alone again. To be alone now seemed intolerable to her. She would leave here and go home to Philadelphia.

. . . It was still raining in the morning when she came out for breakfast. Jared had already prepared it, table set, orange juice waiting, bacon brown and an omelet turned in the pan.

"The skies are cruel," he complained, "but it's just as well, perhaps. I must get back to the lab. I was going to steal another day, fight my conscience, but now there's no need. You're tired?"

"A little—no, not tired, just muscle sore."

"Just as well we can't be tempted."

They ate again almost in silence and she wondered, with a slight resentment, if he were on guard. After all, she had not kissed him. On the contrary! But they were both formal this gray morning.

"Shall you be staying long?" he asked when, breakfast over, he prepared to leave.

"No, I am leaving, perhaps tomorrow," she replied.

46

Then, resentment still alive, she added, "I shall probably stop on the way for a few days with an old friend, Edwin Steadley."

He heard this coldly. "Well, good-bye," he said. Then added somewhat gracelessly, she thought, "Of course we'll meet again."

"Why not?" she said.

"In the course of human events," Edwin said, "I cannot live much longer. I do not come of long-lived ancestry, and ancestry seems to count, in the matters of life and death. Already I have lived longer than my parents were able to do. My mother died at sixty-four, surviving my father by three years. He was five years younger than she. Their relationship was a strange one. In some ways he was like a son."

"I shouldn't like such a relationship," she said with decision.

"Ah," he said, "that's because you have such an old lover. I could almost be your grandfather. But the truth is, my darling, that young men don't really know how to love a woman. A young man thinks first of possessing a woman for himself—that is, of impregnating her. At my age a man knows this is impossible, and so he gives himself up to pure love of the woman, without thought of himself. He contemplates her with delight, as I contemplate you. He gives her joy insofar as she accepts his touch, which now is skilled, but in all such matters he thinks only of her. My dear, by the light of the moon, which by some heavenly magic shines at this moment upon your bed, your beautiful body looks like a statue of pale gold. What a fortunate man I am to be thus admitted to your private chamber!"

"I can't understand how it happened," she said, smiling up at him through the mist of her fair hair, loose upon the pillows.

"I had the courage to ask," he replied.

"You asked very confidently," she said, laughing. "I

can't discern any lack of courage in you. But how is it that I had the courage to accept and how is it that it does not seem strange, and certainly not wrong, that you are here? I have never taken a lover before. Therefore why now?"

"A need to give all and to accept all," he said.

"And why am I not in the least shy?" she asked him with genuine wonder.

"We are one," he replied. "Our minds were one, first, and then it became necessary that the oneness be complete."

"And will it continue?"

"Until I feel death come near. When that moment occurs, I will let you know. Don't try to stay me or comfort me. I must prepare for the solitary passing. I shall need all my strength for it. Therefore—"

Here he paused so long that, moved to tenderness, she drew him into her arms.

"Are you afraid?" she asked.

But he would not accept pity, even a tender pity. He loosed himself from her and leaned over her, smoothing her long hair from her forehead, and looked down into her eyes. Upon the bedside table the flame of the candle wavered in a slight breeze from the open window so that light and shadow played upon her face.

"I am not afraid," he told her. "But I have something to say to you, and I want it said now, while I am able to speak the full truth of what I feel. Who knows what it will be when the end draws near? I may be dazed with pain. I may be faint. Death may overtake me in one instant and give me no time. Tell me, my love, are you at peace now? For this moment? We are quite alone in my old house. I sent the housekeeper home—it was some family anniversary—and Henry is away for a short holiday. No one is under this roof except the two of us. We may never again be quite so alone. May I tell you what I want you to know and to remember as long as you live?"

48

"Tell me," she said.

He lay down beside her then, not touching her now except that he took her left hand and held it clasped in both his hands on his breast. Upon inexplicable impulse she had taken off her marriage rings tonight when she washed, and now, caressing her hand, he noticed it was ringless.

"You need not have taken off your rings, my love," he said, and put her hand to his lips.

"I don't know why I did," she said somewhat faintly.

"An instinct," he said.

"Of guilt?" she asked.

"Of honor," he said, "but quite unnecessary. Love is never guilty. It comes to us, always to be welcomed, from whatever source, at whatever time. One love does not displace another. Each love is added richness."

"But could I have accepted your love—as I do—if—" She paused and he carried the question to answer.

"If Eloise, my wife, and Arnold, your husband, had been alive? I would have expressed it differently, you would have accepted it differently. We would not be lying here in the naked moonlight. It would not have been necessary as it now is, to me at least, and I think to you, or you would not have accepted me. As it is, I, because I feel death near, you, because death struck into your house, we feel the necessity of bodily contact before the final parting comes, as it must, my darling! So let me say what I want to say."

"Tell me—"

He drew a deep breath, he closed his eyes, he began, her hand still clasped in both his hands upon his breast.

"I want to tell you how I love you. I want to tell you now, while I am still fully alive, while my brain is clear, while my heart beats, while I have words upon my tongue. *I love you*. I have always loved you. I loved you before I ever knew you, before we ever met.

49

I loved you because I knew the sort of woman I would always love, must always love, and when I saw you, I knew you were she. Of course I love your body because it is yours and because it pleases me. But I love your body because your spirit dwells there, because your incomparable brain is housed in your beautiful skull, because your soul is enshrined in your heart. I cannot imagine your body apart from the essential you. But I cannot imagine the essential you otherwise housed. You are entire in your whole being. I love the least part of you—your long free hair, your hands and feet, your adorable breasts, your waist, your thighs, the way you walk and carry your head. I love your voice, the look in your eyes—have you an idea how your soul speaks through your eyes? No, don't answer! I have more to say. If you had not let me love you—did you observe that I never ask you to love me?—I would have been afraid to descend solitary to the grave. As it is, my love for you sustains me. I fear nothing. I march to the unknown with steady step, for I bear in my heart my love for you. Love is the torch that lights my way. 'O Death, where is thy sting? O Grave, where is thy victory?' "

His voice rang out into the night. He put her hand to his lips and held it there. But she drew it gently away, she lifted herself and took his head between her palms and kissed his lips.

"I am honored," she said. "As long as I live, I am honored. I shall never forget—never, never!"

. . . She was at home again. They had parted, she and Edwin, with a new ease. Whatever they had was somehow eternal. All impatience was gone. A profound unity existed between them, maintained by the flow of his letters.

"I shall write to you whenever I like," he had said at the last moment, "but don't feel you must reply. It does me good to put down my thoughts, crystallize them, actually, in my letters to you. I feel they are permanent, once I give them to you. If anything happens to me, if some morning I don't waken, you have the essential man with you always. You may do as you like with me."

With these words, he began a series of letters, which arrived almost daily. Without attempting to reply to these letters she received them, absorbed them, and when she felt the need of communication, she wrote at any hour, day or night, of what at the moment engaged her thoughts, relevant to his or not. He wrote:

"I am astonished that the more I contemplate death the more I am upheld by a new confidence in the persistence of life beyond. This may simply be wishfulness, and yet I think not. Or it may be that, infused by love as I am—thanks to you, my darling—I believe final death is irrational, therefore morally wrong, therefore impossible. I assert the impossibility by a new faith in immortality. It is not for myself that I make the assertion. It is because of you, whom I love as perfection, that I insist it is morally wrong that the creation of perfection end in mere dust. Somehow the entire being cannot be thus dependent on a temporary manifestation, namely, the human frame, composite of water and a handful of chemicals. The ability to love must surely have a significance, must surely contain a promise. Without love, it is easy to believe that death is final, but with it—impossible! The very will to believe suggests persistence."

To this she replied:

"Spring is here. The old maple trees, which seemed to me as a child already as old as eternity, are clothed in tender green. My house is rich with early roses. The gardener specializes in a certain few flowers, and roses are one of the few. In the midst of all this color and glory, your letter is like music, or perhaps, better, a voice, putting into words the promise of immortal spring. Though winter intervenes, life begins again in spring. As for me, I am idle, simply enjoying, not

51

thinking very much, too lazy even to visit friends. They visit me. I tolerate them affectionately but without enthusiasm. I am happy in myself."

This was not entirely true, she realized, even as she sealed the letter and sent it off. In the midst of the ordered daily life, she was aware of a secret restlessness, a query she did not pursue. The air was still cool. No wind, no storm, disturbed the golden air. Never had the house seemed so comfortable, the grounds so encompassing, the smooth lawns clipped of early growth, the shrubbery controlled, the trees in bud and leaf. Yet in the midst of all this to which she was accustomed she was waiting for something more and, moreover, was aware of waiting.

She had received one short note from Jared Barnow, thanking her for letting him stay in her Vermont house. She had not answered it. Why should she, indeed? A casual hospitality, a casual note of thanks, an invitation casually given, a half promise of acceptance—all in all, but there was no more here than gossamer. She must understand herself. Loneliness was inevitable and not to be assuaged by one who merely passed by. She must busy herself, first with the house. It was now hers alone. It could be changed, improved, made new. After all, a house should change with changing generations, become the setting for a new personality.

A new personality? Herself—no other! She could be a different person now, someone she had not known, less shy, less retiring, more concerned with her looks, with her mind—in short, with growth. Arnold in his own way had been a retreat. In the shelter of his superior age, his success as a famous lawyer, she had felt no stimulus except to be what he wished her to be, his wife, the mother of intelligent and reasonably obedient children, a charming hostess, a figure conventionally correct in the conventional and correct society of an old conservative city. She had felt no great desire to be any other than this, for Arnold had not restrained her. She had not been aware of ambition unfulfilled and on the whole she had enjoyed her state of being. She knew that Arnold in his own fashion had loved her more than she loved him, but she had loved him, nevertheless, without regret, and she supposed their relationship was one common to persons in their life circumstances.

Now, however, it occurred to her that she might be quite a different person and a creeping curiosity beset her. Suppose, indeed, that she became someone entirely new? Suppose she began by doing what she wanted to do, saying what she wanted to say, going where she wanted to go? She could not define as yet such yearnings, but then she was accustomed to being as she was. Suppose, she told herself, suppose she studied her own desires as they might appear, once they were allowed? It occurred to her that she was in fact repressed, although unaware of repression. The house, for example. If she could not think of what she wanted, she could begin by rejecting what she did not want.

Walking thoughtfully about the vast rooms, looking at one object and another, it slowly came to her that she did not want any of it. It was not at all her idea of a house for herself. Grandparents and parents had built it, had filled it with the furniture of their own age, valuable, heavy, immovable. She would sell it—no, she would give it away, fill it with orphans or old men and women, homeless people whom it could shelter as it had sheltered her.

How did one rid one's self of a shelter? And where would one build again? And what should she build, what could she build, when she did not know what she was? Or wanted to be! To Edwin she was a woman he loved and by so loving prolonged his life. To Jared Barnow she was nothing, perhaps scarcely an acquaintance. Suddenly she remembered her decision. She would do whatever she wanted to do—that was what she had decided. But she must do it quickly before decision faded into old sheltering ways. Now she must do it. She crossed three rooms swiftly and in the dim old library she sat down at her grandfather's mahogany desk and wrote a brief letter.

Dear Jared Barnow:
 I don't like my house any more. I am tired of it.
I want to build a new one. But what? Here is a
chance for invention, is it not?

She searched for and found his note with his address. She would mail the letter when she went to luncheon with Amelia Darwent, next door. But at the mailbox, holding the letter in her hand, she changed her mind. What would he think? She put the letter in her purse and snapped it shut.

"But why build another house?" Amelia inquired.

They were at luncheon, the two of them in the oval dining room. Amelia, an only child, continued to live in the great old house on a large corner lot on the Main Line, in the midst of twenty acres of land, which was what remained of three thousand acres, presented to her ancestors in the days of William Penn as a reward for favors now forgotten. She sat, slim and erect, her hair becomingly silvery, in her usual place at the rounded end of the table. Rose, the Irish maid, a desiccated, elderly Rose, served them.

"Because I want to rid myself of old encumbrances," Edith said.

"You can't rid yourself of an inheritance," Amelia persisted. She tasted her clear soup and looked at Rose reproachfully. "It's not hot!"

"On account, madame, you didn't come when called," Rose said truculently.

"Oh, well—"

Amelia lifted her bouillon cup and drank the soup as though it were coffee.

"What's next?" she inquired.

"Broiled squab, like you said, madame," Rose replied.

"Put it on the table," Amelia ordered. "Serve the salad, and leave us."

"Yes, madame."

Alone with Amelia, she unfolded her plan of a house, a place not yet clear in her own mind.

"I met a young man——"

"Aha," Amelia said triumphantly. "I thought so! You look ten years younger. There's nothing so absolutely cosmetic for a woman as a young man, or so I am told."

"Amelia, you are repulsive," she said severely.

"My dear, when were we not honest with each other?" Amelia demanded. "You are looking unnaturally beautiful—and have—ever since you returned from Vermont."

"Amelia, will you stop?"

"Don't pretend then, Edie!"

The two women looked at one another over the low silver bowl filled with small pink hothouse roses. Amelia's black eyes were laughing and Edith turned her own blue eyes away.

"I don't know why I tolerate you, Amelia Darwent."

"Because you know I never tell anyone what you tell me, Edith Chardman!"

"There's nothing to tell," Edith said. She put out her hand and touched a rose. "I can't see why your roses are always better than mine."

"Bone meal," Amelia said. "So what has the young man to do with the house?"

"Nothing," Edith said. She helped herself to a squab.

"Nothing," Amelia repeated.

55

"Except I'll ask him for suggestions," she amended. "But that's nothing."

"Then let's not talk about him," Amelia retorted. "Let's talk about you. You're someone to talk about! My dear, how shall you amuse yourself?"

"By building the house, of course."

"But where?"

"Somewhere—by the sea."

She was improvising as she went. She had not thought of a house by the sea, but the moment she spoke the words, she knew that of course it was what she had wanted for years. She had even spoken of it to Arnold once, long ago, but he had refused the idea.

"That surf, pounding all night! We'd not be able to sleep."

"You'd not be able to sleep," she had retorted. "I'd be lulled."

"You can sleep anywhere," he said with one of his wry smiles, never unkind and yet edged. He was always the superior male, an attitude that she attributed to the combination of English and German elements in the ancestry, dating from the marriage of an early English great-grandfather with a German *Mädchen*. Environment had encouraged these ancestral traits. He had not even been overly impressed by her Phi Beta Kappa key, won in her senior year at Radcliffe. It would take time for her to recover from the atmospheric pressure of her marriage.

As if she had divined these thoughts, Amelia now spoke.

"Do you know, I am quite curious about you, Edith."

"Why?" she asked.

"Arnold kept such a strict hand." Amelia was vigorously salting and peppering her salad. "I shall be watching you, lovingly, of course, for I am very fond of you, to see just how you will blossom. For I don't doubt you'll blossom, my dear, with the charming looks

56

you have. There are young men who actually prefer women over forty. Oh, yes, there are—don't look so surprised!"

"Do I look surprised?" she inquired.

"Shocked, perhaps," Amelia said.

For an instant she pondered whether to confide in Amelia, that old friend, the astounding news of her unexpected new relationship with Edwin. Immediately she decided against it. She had never been given to confidences and, moreover, she was certain that Amelia would not be able to comprehend the quality of the relationship. Amelia would laugh, or Amelia would make ribald comments about lecherous old men, comments that would indeed apply, doubtless, to most old men, but not to a man as intelligent, as learned, as wise, as Edwin Steadley. To Amelia love was sex, whatever others might call it. Instead of confidence she replied with mild evasion.

"I am not aware of any great changes about to take place in me."

A monstrous lie she realized as soon as she had spoken, for it remained incredible that she had accepted Edwin, had actually allowed him in her bed, thereby in that simple act asserting independence of the past years during which she had known intimately no man except her husband. And it was not to be explained to anyone, even to herself, why the intimacy with Edwin, at once fulfilled and unfulfilled, was no infidelity to Arnold, living or dead.

"Each experience of love," Edwin had said one night in the darkness, "is a life in itself. Each has nothing to do with what has taken place before or will take place again. Love is born, it pursues its separate way, world without end, transmuted into life energy."

"I doubt I shall ever love anyone else," she had replied in the darkness. At that moment she had deeply loved the beautiful old man. Never had she known such a mind as his, crystalline in purity. That was the amazing quality. Even when he held her against him, the quality was not changed. She had loved Arnold, too, but he was divided, the one man intelligent, though not creatively so, a decisive, calculating self-confident man whom she admired and trusted, and the other a silent, possessively passionate man, who appeared regularly and without preliminaries in her bedroom to fulfill his primary need. She could not imagine talking in the night with Arnold about life and death and what communication might be possible between them. Arnold took it for granted that death was total end.

"I see a change in you already," Amelia now declared, dipping her fingers in a Venetian glass finger bowl.

"Tell me what you see."

Thus encouraged, Amelia lit a long taper-thin cigar and proceeded. "Well, you are less restrained, more unconscious of yourself, even in the way you walk."

"I suppose I was always unconsciously conscious of being Arnold's wife."

"He criticized you too much." Amelia's tone conveyed dislike of Arnold.

"Not really. He was always gentle with me."

Amelia laughed. "As gentle as iron!"

"Perhaps I needed iron," she replied mildly.

She decided within herself that she did not like Amelia as much as she had supposed, or perhaps it was that now, living alone and without Arnold to return to for masculine relief, Amelia seemed aggressive and overpowering. She must not, she reflected as Amelia led the way to the drawing room, fall into the mistake of becoming involved with women friends and their ever-narrowing interests in themselves and each other. She must take up an intellectual pursuit, she must discover an individual activity, alone and for herself. It seemed to her at this moment that the new house, built entirely for herself alone, satisfied the immediate answer to the question. But what intellectual pursuit, what mental activity? She remained in Amelia's house for another half hour, however, her usual graceful, amiable self, that self which Arnold had so admired and, of course, had loved.

"My dear," he had said more than once, "it is pleasant to live with a quiet woman, and one also beautifully serene."

It occurred to her that she would miss such remarks when she had time to do so. Just now Edwin's letters, arriving almost daily, took their place. Arnold's letters, in their rare moments of separation, had not been at all like Edwin's.

"I really must go, Amelia," she said.

"What can you possibly now have to make you hurry away?" Amelia demanded.

She gave Amelia her somewhat absent smile as she rose. "There's always one thing or another," she said vaguely, and left.

. . . The new house now took possession of her. She was glad she had not mailed the letter to Jared, for had she done so she would have shared the house already, somehow. Instead she had taken the letter from her purse and torn it up when she came home from the luncheon with Amelia. Nonexistent though the house was, she was already living in it. The next morning, sitting at the writing table in the library, she was not even impatient for the mail. When the houseman delivered it to her on a silver tray, she saw on top a thick envelope, addressed in Edwin's surprisingly bold handwriting, but she did not, as usual, open it immediately. Instead she finished the wing to the new house, now taking form in a plan drawn on a large sheet of paper. Then she opened the letter.

"My dear," he began exactly as though he had not left off, "it now occurs to me that death has at least one important use. There is no human progress without death. Life is never static and thus inevitably it progresses from youth to old age. But the old become too wise, too prudent, and therefore life must begin over and over again in the young, if there is to be progress. For the young do not know enough to be prudent and therefore they attempt the impossible—and achieve it, generation after generation. You see I am seeking excuses to die! I admit it. When you are not here, I feel myself dying. I ought to die. It is time. But I cling to you, my darling. I prolong myself through love. And yet, upon further reflection, I realize that I myself need to die, in order that my life may be complete and whole. It is only when I have end as well as beginning that my individuality is definite. When I say *I,* it means as a human being. No, I am wrong. Since you opened to me the door of your room, I am set apart from all others against common sense. Time has become my most treasured commodity. 'You must live long enough to see her again'—this is what I tell my body every night when I lay it down to sleep. It is still necessary that I live, although death waits, impatient."

She read the letter carefully to the end, then folded its pages, put them in the envelope and slipped the envelope into a secret drawer and locked it with a combination. Her servants, as curious as any now that Arnold was dead and she was, so to speak, alone, would not be averse to reading a letter upon the envelope of which was written so blackly the name of a man. This done, she took up her drawing pencil. As Edwin had written, it was necessary to live, and for her, too, it was necessary. And since it was necessary, what more logical than that she should have the sort of house she wanted to live in? For she realized that she had never had that house. This vast structure now surrounding her, its twenty-two rooms spreading over acreage, was merely the house in which she had been born, and in which she and Arnold had lived, with their two children.

The house in Vermont, too, had not been built for her alone. No, she wanted a house where there was no place for anyone except herself alone. She could go to Edwin, and would go to him when and if she chose, but he could never come to her and so there was no need to make a place for him. She would slip into his life occasionally and slip away again. As for her children, they had their own houses, into which she might or might not go as she pleased, and they had no need of a place in her house. Need there be even a guest room? Her mind flew to that snowy night when Jared Barnow stood at her door. What if he appeared again? But if he never appeared, a room for him would be a waste. Or, for that matter, there was always this huge house, its beautiful rooms empty, and she would simply return here to receive him. She had settled it. She would not have a guest room. The house would be entirely her own. Instead of a guest-room wing, she would have a sunken garden.

. . . It was perhaps a week later that the telephone rang just before midnight. She had worked ever since her solitary, eight o'clock dinner, drawing in meticulous detail the rooms of her house. Merely because she would be alone in it did not mean it would have only a few rooms, not at all. She wanted her interests separated by walls and spaces, the library separated from the music room, and especially she wanted a contemplation room whose semicircular windows encompassed the sea. She could not imagine how she would furnish this room, but when the time came she would know—and of course there must be the usual rooms for sleep and food and service, but where she dined must be open to gardens and where she slept must be open to the stars.

In the midst of total absorption she heard the muted telephone ringing persistently. Her daughter, she supposed, who, married long before Arnold died, made it a habit to call late at night, on the supposition that her mother lived a life violently social, whereas the fact was that she lived almost as a recluse, making excuse that she had not recovered from Arnold's death. Thus prepared to hear Millicent's high and silvery voice, she was unprepared to hear quite another, an impetuous baritone which she instantly recognized as belonging to Jared Barnow.

"It's fearfully late, I apologize, but my little plane is grounded—something wrong in the engine—and it just occurs to me that this city, which has always been for me an adjunct to the airport, is in reality the place where you live. I could take a room at a hotel. On the other hand—"

He broke off expectantly and she quickly filled in the pause.

"Of course, come here. Have you dined?"

"Yes, in some other city. I'm due in New York tomorrow, but I don't wish to go ahead and leave my little machine alone, not until I know what's wrong. I don't like tinkering strangers."

"Come along, then. You'll take a cab, of course—and the man will know the way. You have the address?"

"Do you think I could forget it? I'll be there. Sure you're not in bed?"

"I am here, respectably clothed and in my library."

He laughed and hung up.

She sat thoughtful for moments. The day had turned chill in the deceptive early summer and she heard a spatter of rain against the wide glass doors that led to the east terrace. The fire was laid as usual in the great chimney piece and she rose and touched a match. No, she decided, she would not change her gown. She had chosen this one for herself, a green silk, a soft material and easy in its cut. Part of her new independence was choosing her garments for herself. Arnold had never liked green, her favorite color, the color of life and springtime and youthfulness of spirit, and the apple green of this gown was the one she liked best among the many shades of green. And then, to signify her new indifference, a manifestation of independence, she went back to the writing table upon which the plan of her house was taking form, and began to work as though he had not called.

She was absorbed enough, in spite of a secret excitement which she suppressed, so that in less than a hour, when he appeared at the door of the library, whither he had been ushered by her previous order, she forgot the intervening time.

"How good to see you," he exclaimed, holding out both his hands for hers.

"Thank you for thinking of me when your plane came down," she said, aware that he was holding her hands firmly, aware of his dark eyes warmly upon her, aware of his smile, frankly joyous. He was taller, younger, more sophisticated than she remembered him in ski clothes. She was acutely aware of his arm about her shoulders as they walked to the chairs by the fire and she drew herself gently away from his grasp and was shocked to discover herself uncertain as to how to proceed, confused merely by his touch. How stupid of me, she thought, as if so slight a gesture today had any meaning! She seated herself opposite him, unable to think of what to say, and so said nothing, but smiled at him, whereupon he began.

"I must say this is a different setting for you, and very becoming. I like these great old houses. One doesn't see them very often. Is it lonely for you here?"

She shook her head. "I have enough to do."

"What, for example?"

She was not prepared, however, to tell him about the new house and she replied lightly. "Oh, music, friends, books, or just—reorganizing myself for a new life."

"No worthy causes and so forth?"

"A few charities my husband was interested in, and in which I am not."

"I can't see you a lady bountiful."

She maneuvered the conversation away from herself, which was easily done, for he was staring into the fire as though for moments he forgot her and she did not wish to be forgotten.

"Tell me what you are doing now. I've only thought of a skier."

He came back to her. "I? Well, I came here to see a man who lives not too far away—a scientist—engineer fellow, who dreams of combining the disciplines to focus them on medical problems. Doctors, especially surgeons, are extraordinarily old-fashioned in technological ways. They keep on using antiquated tools—you wouldn't believe—well, the idea of modernizing medical, especially surgical, instruments through the new engineering techniques fascinates me. I'm a bit of an idealist, I daresay. It gives me satisfaction to imagine that an invention of mine might save a life instead of just adding gold to the coffers of a multimillionaire—or blowing someone on the other side of the world to bits."

She was not prepared for this sudden submersion into his thinking and she had no wish to pretend to understand what he was talking about. Her own defense against this new and all but overpowering awareness of his physical being was to comprehend his mind, his swiftly moving, brilliant, perhaps moody mind, as she vaguely surmised. It occurred to her now that she was beginning to see dimly the real man, not the young skier who came out of the snows and into her house in the mountains of Vermont. He was looking about the room now and restlessly, as though in search, and suddenly he shivered.

"Have you something I could drink—something burning hot? I've caught cold up there in the upper regions. Stupidly I forgot to bring an extra jacket."

"Of course," she said, and touched a button. "I don't think Weston is upstairs yet."

Her elderly houseman came at her call and she spoke to him in her usual kindly but distant fashion.

"Weston, Mr. Barnow is catching cold. Can you make him something hot?"

"Certainly, madame," the man replied.

"And, Weston, I suppose the green room is ready for guests?"

"Always, madame."

"Turn down the bed for Mr. Barnow, will you?"

"Certainly, madame. Will Mr. Barnow be here for breakfast?"

"Yes—and perhaps longer."

"Very well. Thank you, madame." He made his old-fashioned bow and went away.

"This is your setting," Jared said.

"Ah, you don't know me," she replied.

"No? But I shall, in time!"

"Is there time? You are young and very busy. And I have—dreams of my own."

"I must be in them."

He made the declaration boldly, so confident of her approval that in herself she felt withdrawal, almost distaste, even while she was aware again of his physical beauty. She withdrew from that, too, abruptly.

"Tell me what you meant a moment ago when you spoke of combining disciplines."

He was leaning back in his easy chair, his hands clasped behind his head, his eyes closed. Now he sat up abruptly and opened his eyes.

"What do you know about medical engineering?" he inquired.

"Nothing," she said promptly. "It must be something new, since my father's time."

"Relatively new," he agreed.

"Then please be simple."

He laughed. "Simply, then, it's this: the medical men

have been and are extraordinarily backward in the new disciplines of mathematics, physics and engineering. Yet they are working with life systems, without enough of the research that is essential if they are to do their work successfully. The very instruments upon which they depend for accuracy of diagnosis and healing are often so old-fashioned as to be obsolete. Medical scientists are becoming aware of this and some universities are creating departments of bio-medical engineering. But that's a neither-fish-nor-fowl sort of thing so far, in my opinion, only creating men for jobs that won't exist after a few years. I have a different approach to such interdisciplinary activity and that's what I wanted to talk to this fellow about. He's a pioneer in the field. I wish your father were alive. He'd be the one I'd be seeing first."

"He'd like you," she said.

"And I'd have worshipped at his feet! There's no mind alive today that equals his. Why do the great ones die young?"

"Trying to save the world," she replied. "He was on his way to Japan, to help the Japanese rebuild the cyclotron we destroyed during the world war."

"I know. I read about it," he said.

There was a knock at the door and Weston appeared with a tall mug of steaming liquid.

"Toddy, sir," he said in his high old voice.

"Thanks," Jared said, and taking the glass he sipped its contents. "Ah, that's good. It goes straight into my bones."

"Yes, sir. Good night, sir. Good night, madame. Everything is in order."

"Thank you, Weston, and good night."

The door closed behind him and they were silent. Jared sipped the toddy, his mind absent, as she could see, and she did not try again to recall him. She sat quietly looking at him while he gazed into the fire, sipping until the mug was empty. Then he set it down and turned to her apologetically.

"Forgive me. I'm not a good guest tonight. When I have a problem on my mind—"

She interrupted him. "But I understand. I shouldn't like you to feel as though you had to entertain me. I was thinking, myself."

"Of what?"

Impossible to say the truth—"Of you!" She was too shy for that bold truth. She spoke lightly and rose from the chair.

"I was thinking you should go to your bed and sleep away your cold. Your room is the first door on the right, at the head of the stairs. If you find you need anything in the night, press the button on the telephone that says W. It connects with Weston's room."

"What a palace," he said. He had risen when she rose and now he stood tall above her, and looked down upon her, smiling, and she looked up at him, uncertain of what was next. It was he who decided, abruptly and frankly.

"Do you mind if I kiss you?"

She shook her head, but was speechless, helpless in absurd shyness. A kiss was meaningless, a kiss was nothing nowadays, a kiss could be no more than a casual gift to one's hostess. Ah, but it took two, one to give, one to receive! She felt his lips on her right cheek, and then lightly, very lightly, he turned her head with his two palms, and she felt his lips upon hers, a quick brush of warmth.

"Good night," he said. "What time is breakfast?"

"Whenever you like," she said, as casually as though there had not been this kiss which lay upon her lips a living coal.

"When do you breakfast?" he demanded at the door.

"At nine o'clock."

"Good heavens, what a lie-abed!"

67

He pretended to be shocked and she laughed.

"Good night," she called as he mounted the stairs. "Sleep well in that room! It was mine when I was a girl."

She was sleepless for hours that night, and when she woke it was nearly ten o'clock the next morning. Her first thought was of him and she rang the kitchen. Weston answered.

"Has Mr. Barnow breakfasted?" she asked.

"Yes, madame, at eight o'clock sharp and left immediately, begging your pardon. He wrote you a note, madame—I put it on the breakfast table for you."

She hung up, blaming herself. How could she have slept away the last hour of his presence? She made haste to shower and dress and, taking her seat at the table in the sunny breakfast room, she found his note under her plate.

"I am sorry to leave in this discourteous fashion, but I had an early call from the man I came to see. I am to meet him at nine o'clock in his laboratory. I have barely time to make it. My plane will be ready at noon. I shall be flying back to you one of these days. Here is my telephone number—and my thanks. Wonderful to see you again! Jared."

She studied the handwriting. It was large and firm and very black.

. . . Summer moved into misdummer. Or was it only she who so lazily moved? In this first summer since Arnold's death—he had died in the autumn of last year—she found herself given over to a lassitude that was far from empty. Indeed, it seemed to her that she had never enjoyed so richly the sensuous air, the scintillating clarity of sunshine, the lush glory of the flowers and foliage. Since she had not yet fulfilled the year of traditional mourning for her husband she had excuse to decline all invitations she did not wish to accept and to accept only those she did not wish to decline. Once or twice a week she went out to dinner or luncheon with some old friend of hers or Arnold's, and on the intervening days she cleared from the house the last of Arnold's personal possessions, his clothes, his pipes, his papers. When this was done, she took up her music again, and seriously, so that several hours a day were occupied at the piano, and other hours were spent in reading books.

She was only beginning to realize now that Arnold had absorbed her life, not purposely but quite naturally and always gently, or perhaps she had been too yielding in allowing herself to be thus absorbed. At any rate, she found a number of small desires to be fulfilled, certain garments, certain colors she had always wanted to wear and for which Arnold had expressed distaste; certain arrangements of the furniture which he had not approved, he being constitutionally opposed to change; even certain foods to which she had been tempted and which he had declared indigestible. Each liberty she now took for herself released her further until she no longer questioned anything she chose to do, as she had done instinctively and by long habit in the first months after Arnold's death.

"You have changed," her son told her on one of his rare and unexpected visits. He lived in Washington with his young wife and their only child, a junior executive in some government department leading to service abroad. She was never quite used to his seemingly sudden development from a sandy-haired rather prosaic little boy to a sandy-haired rather prosaic young man. He had been a good little boy and was now a good young man, touchingly so, she felt at this moment, when his honest blue eyes were fixed affectionately upon her. He had "dropped by," as he put it, one day in early July, on his way to New York, where he was to meet a minor dignitary from some foreign country.

"How have I changed?" she asked half playfully.

"You look rested—and interested again."

"Interested in what, Tony?"

"How should I know? Life, I suppose."

"I am learning to live alone, that's all."

He leaned over her and kissed her cheek in farewell, glancing at his watch. "Now don't you get lonely. Fay and I and the baby can always run up for a few days. Pity that Millicent lives so far away!"

She parried Tony's suggestion.

"Oh, no—thank you, dear. I must learn to live my own life."

"Well, let us know—"

He was off and she relapsed into indolence. She sauntered to the terrace upon which the drawing room opened and stretched herself upon a long chair. Indolent, yes, but a productive indolence, she told herself, sorting out life and feeling—feeling as she had not explored feeling since adolescence. The sun, warm upon her skin, enlivened her blood and yet infused it with delicious languor. And why, she inquired of herself, did she continue to dream of another house, a house of her own, when here she was the heir to beauty long inherited? From where she lay, she could see, and did appreciate, the vistas of clean-cut lawn, tended shrubbery and vast old trees, culminating at a distance in a quiet pool, a fountain, the marble figure of a Grecian woman, installed by her grandfather when these acres, this house, were his inheritance.

This remembrance of Jared, which never left her, quickened into sharp longing of which she was half ashamed. Had he not come so suddenly, had he not left so abruptly, had he not been obsessed by a dream of his own, a dream that obviously had nothing to do with her, had he, in short, visited her wholeheartedly, with whatever intention she could not imagine, then would he not have lingered here, have been beside her in another chair as comfortable as this one in which she lay, warmed by the sun and made languid by beauty?

She was too experienced a woman not to comprehend the danger into which she was moving, and more than anger, for it was also absurdity. She would not allow herself to fall in love with a man years younger than herself. Years? Decades—

"Madame, the telephone, please. Person to person," Weston said at the door.

She rose at once. Of course it was Edwin.

"My love," his kind old voice said at her ear. "I find it impossible to live any longer without a sight of you. Are you completely obligated to others or dare I suggest a little visit? If it were possible, how gladly I would come to you! Legs could do it, but my heart, an ancient valve, cries danger. I don't want to become a sudden invalid in your house, although for me it would have pleasant aspects."

She was not quite prepared for so sudden a move. There was another presence now in her house. On the other hand, might it not be a protection against that invading presence, a reminder of age and dignity, if she visited Edwin for a few days?

"Let me think about it," she told him. "If I can arrange things—"

He intervened with urgency. "There is no one to think of now except yourself, is there? And possibly a bit about me? The old heart ticktocks away, but it reminds me that it won't go on forever."

She laughed. "Shame on you! Blackmailing me!"

"Of course! All's fair in love—"

"I'll call you tonight."

"I shan't sleep until you do."

Thus they parted and she was alone again, yet not alone, for she realized in this instant that she might never be alone again unless she could recover from the new presence in her thoughts. However she strove to think of other places, other people, the activities of her daily life, her delights of which she had many, her duties and absorptions accumulated through years of

71

living in the same city, the same house, the new presence of Jared pervaded. In dawning panic she felt the need to escape, and how better to escape than to hasten to Edwin and, devoting herself to him, drive out that other?

Without waiting for nightfall upon decision she fled to the telephone and called. "Edwin, I have arranged everything. I will come tomorrow. I'll drive myself and arrive in time to dine with you."

"Blessed be tomorrow, darling—and blessed be you for answering my need!"

His voice was bright with joy and she was made hopeful. Let her be satisfied in comforting one who needed her rather than dwelling upon her own need! And what, for that matter, was her need? In reality, what was it, brutally put, but an incipient and dangerous infatuation, the consequence, in all probability, of her solitary life? For she was still unready to resume her old life of luncheons and dinners and such engagements, and uncertain indeed of ever resuming them and, in this uncertainty, inclined to new interests to be sought and defined, but assuredly not in the person of a young invader, a chance acquaintance who, if pursued or allowed to pursue, might threaten the entire structure of her reasonable and dignified life. Escape she must, therefore, and in the spirit of one seeking escape, she left the house early the next day after a restless moonlit night and was well on her way by midmorning.

It was a happy thought to drive herself in the small convertible car, concentration preventing the thoughts from which she was in flight. Speed and motion, the wind blowing back her hair, for she had put down the top of the car, gave the illusion of actual escape. A few days with Edwin would set her right, bring her back to reality. She would take shelter in the safety of his love for her and love him, as indeed she did, too, but quietly and with the respect due his age and great fame. Let her be honored by love and not roused by it—although perhaps she had made a mistake in allowing him to come to her room? Yes, it was a mistake. Tonight she would tell him so.

"Edwin, my dear," she would begin. "We are past the age, you and I, when we need the physical expression of love. If others knew of it, they would construe it wrongly. It might even be shocking to them. Let us therefore be content with good talk and sitting side by side. Dear Edwin—" Here she would pause, here she might take his hand in hers and press it.

In reality, after arriving just in time for dinner in the shadowy dining room lit only by candles in ancient silver candlesticks, and after his rapturous greeting of her, she perceived that he looked thin and somehow pathetic in his loneliness. She put off saying anything that might dampen his joy in her coming, put it off indeed until after dinner and then put it off again because he wanted to talk about the book he was writing on the possibility and impossibility of immortality. He drew her hand through his arm when they rose from the table and directed their steps toward the drawing room, where a wood fire was burning against the chill of evening in the mountains. They seated themselves side by side on the settee facing the chimney piece, and he began at once, keeping her left hand on his arm by his covering right hand.

"One can't test one's own thoughts, you know, darling—and I am not at all sure of the validity of the philosophy I am hewing out of this old brain of mine. Is it too soon after dinner to think grave thoughts?"

"Not if you are thinking them," she said, smiling.

He was silent for a long moment, perhaps to collect those thoughts, perhaps to change the playful mood in which they had dined to his usual philosophical searching. Then he began afresh.

"You have had a very profound influence upon me, Edith, and therefore upon my thinking. I have rewritten several chapters in my philosophy which I had thought was permanent. You have brought a new urgency upon me to consider death, its finality, its meaning. I want to prove that death is not final. I want to assure myself that *I* continue because *you* continue. As for others, let them continue if they wish. It is *my* immortality which I must prove and to myself first. Therefore I have been considering death anew. Is it an end, or is it an entrance? But what is this self of mine which can consider death as though it were a state separate from the self? Ah, it's the separateness that is so significant! I contemplate death as though I were continuing after its arrival, exactly as I contemplate it before its arrival. I, therefore, survive since I can contemplate myself afterward as well as before. Is that specious, my darling? Be frank—I urge the truth! Don't let my new anxiety to live beyond the grave lead me into false paths!"

The magic of his beautiful, resonant voice, still strong, persuaded her interest. She was a stranger to philosophy in his sense of the word, and although she had studied philosophy in college, she had read enough since to know that modern philosophy had changed much that was old—Josiah Royce, for example, whose books had been her testaments in her senior year at Radcliffe.

"At least death is an interruption," she suggested now.

"Granted," he said heartily, "but only an interruption. The contemplating self, released from its temporary phase, would proceed to its next activity. Of that I need not speak, for assuredly in any activity you and I would find one another. It is the moment of death that I must analyze, if such analysis is possible. Is this moment only a fraction of time or is it—eternity?" His voice fell to a sudden whisper upon that awesome word.

She considered, deeply thoughtful. "I suppose," she

said at last and hesitating very much, for though she had thought long about Arnold's death, yet she felt humble before this virile old philosopher, "I suppose that one approach might be to limit the definition of death by eliminating what we know it is not. For example, we know that the body returns to dust and is no more in its present components."

"Exactly," he exclaimed triumphantly; "therefore let us eliminate the body. That's used and put aside forever. But what's left, the self—can we go further than to say that at least the idea of its continuance is a reality? Or to put it otherwise, how much of a reality is the mere idea of it? Take atomic energy, released as fission between atomic elements. It existed first as an idea, did it not? It existed, but how much and how long? If the idea were right, then it was real to that degree. If it had been wrong—and ideas can be mistaken and therefore wrong, and therefore unreal—it would have existed briefly or not at all. Yet might it not, for all that, have existed in itself and forever, as an idea? In other words again, the beginning of any reality is contained in an idea."

"Springs from an idea?" she suggested.

He repudiated this. "No, the idea *is* the first reality."

"The possibility of reality," she amended.

"Aha, I've got you!" he cried in triumph. "Then the possibility is in itself a reality, isn't it?"

She pondered and made reply. "But possibility is not continuance!"

"No, but continuance is not entirely negated, so long as there is the possibility of continuance."

She laughed. "So how to get out of this tangle?"

He did not laugh or even smile. Indeed he became intensely serious. Releasing her hand, which all this time he had continued to hold, he seemed to forget her presence.

"By the intuitions," he mused. "If perpetuity is the reality of space, of energy, of atoms themselves, shall it

75

be denied to us, who know our being? I reject the absurdity!"

She listened, enthralled, caught and held in the brilliant outpouring of words and logic and so continued for hours. When at last the clock struck twelve he stopped abruptly. "Good heavens, how I go on! And your angelic patience! Come to bed, my love."

And in her bedazzlement, quite forgetting that she had planned otherwise, she let herself be led away.

. . . In the night she felt herself enfolded and, waking, she found him at her side. In the moonlight she saw his face above her, amazing in its strong beauty. Age revealed the outlines of perfect bone structure, the eyes, still burning bright, were steel blue beneath silvered brows. He had a tender mouth, not small, not large, the lips delicately sculptured, and suddenly she felt them on her own, passionately tender.

"I have been watching my love asleep," he murmured, "so beautiful in sleep, my darling!"

"Have you not slept?" she asked.

"I will not," he replied. "I want to know you are here—every moment I want to know. You give me certainty. I shall survive. I *know,* because I *live!* There is that substance in life which cannot yield to death. Plato was convinced of it, long ago. I have the *right* to live, my beloved. It would be too great an injustice, too irrational a waste, were I to die—I or any other who demands life. Survival *will* be because it *ought* to be. This is the great moral imperative."

Enfolded, uplifted and encouraged, she felt her love for him rise upward as though on wings. She adored him with a sense of worship. His spirit, bold and brave, the ardor of his nature, the brilliance of his mind, piercing beyond knowledge, awed her and gave her protection. If there were one in whom she could put her trust, this was he. She drew him to her, she for the first time the aggressor, and kissed him full upon the mouth, feeling meanwhile delight and pain—delight because she loved him in a way she had not known before, with a pure pleasure, and pain because she must live in this body of hers years beyond him. But now, at this brief moment, brief because it could not be shared beyond the span of years, she felt herself swept clean of every other love. She had loved Arnold but without worship. Indeed, he would have been shy of worship, protested against it, rejected it because it made him uncomfortable. But Edwin had the greatness of simplicity.

"I love you," she told him. "You speak of reality. Well, this is reality. I love you. True, I love you in a way I don't understand, but I love you."

He received this assurance with large calm. "Then we shall meet beyond the grave. The power to love—I to love you is easy enough, my darling, but you to love me, this gives me guarantee. Love pierces through all that is false, all that is ephemeral. Love finds reality, love creates the longing to live forever, and the longing is the promise of immortality. 'He that loveth aright,' Plato tells us, 'is born of the immortal One.' O my darling, thank you!"

He released her, he fell back on his pillow and, breathing a deep sigh of peace, was instantly asleep.

. . . She returned home the next morning and a few weeks passed, three or four, even five, possibly, for she scarcely marked the days. They were peaceful weeks, vaguely happy, vague because she made no effort. Amelia was in Europe for three months, and she had no word from Jared. She was almost grateful for his silence, for it gave her space in which to live with herself alone, to sort herself out, to discover her needs, if she had them, her hopes, if hope was necessary. Friends came to call, to tell her how well she looked, how glad they were that she was recovering sensibly from Arnold's death. She listened, she smiled, she was silent. What she was beginning to understand was that a new self was appearing within her. With the passing of Arnold, a life had passed, her previous life, childhood and girlhood, her young womanhood, her wifehood. All things now were to be made new, what and how she did not know, but the cause was in herself, the cause and the source. She must wait for the self to unfold.

Meanwhile she worked on the plans for her house. In the mornings after her late breakfast, she worked, planning every detail, every color, every device. She was a good mathematician, and she used a slide rule skillfully. She would be her own architect, and soon she would go in search of a site. Then she would find a contractor. And this old house in which she still lived, what would become of it? Give it away? Sell it? With it she would be selling a lifetime of memories. That decision, too, must wait. She was not sure yet of her own destiny. She brooded often and long upon her new self, and this brooding separated her from the past. More than a house must be planned. A woman must live in the new house. Would she live alone?

She was in the library one morning, thus meditating, while she glanced over her mail. Still no word from Jared, but then he never wrote letters. If he wanted communication it would be by telegram or telephone. There was, however, a letter from Edwin. She was not quite sure from the handwriting on the envelope. It was sprawling and uncertain, not like Edwin's surprisingly firm, black writing. But it was from him, as she perceived when she opened it, a few lines straggling off into nothingness.

"O my darling, the change has come! I am stricken. 'Te morituri salutamus.' It is I who am about to die—I alone. I die, as I have lived, in the faith that we shall meet again—"

That was all—no explanation, no description, simply he was dying. She started to her feet, but the tele-

78

phone, ringing suddenly and sharply, stayed her. She took the receiver and heard a man's voice.

"Mrs. Chardman?"

"I am she."

"This is Stephen Steadley. You are a friend of my father. He has asked me to tell you. He is dying. It is a matter of a few days, perhaps hours."

"I opened his letter just a few minutes ago and I was afraid—"

"Everything is being done. It's his heart, of course. We are all here, my brothers, my sister and I—the doctors."

"Is he conscious?"

"Very much so. Very interested in the process of dying, in spite of—difficulties."

"Pain?"

"Yes, but he refused sedation. He wants to know, he says—"

His voice broke and she liked him for it. "You know we have been very close—friends," she said.

"He adores you. We've all been so grateful that you broke through his profound loneliness. None of us could do it."

"He broke through mine, too."

It was all she could say. She could not ask the question, Shall I come? She could not ask it of herself. She saw him lying on the bed, that beautiful dying body, stretched in death.

"Good-bye," she said softly.

"Good-bye?" his son repeated, surprised. "Oh, yes, well, I'll let you know immediately."

Immediately Edwin dies, she thought, but said nothing, her voice choked with tears. She put up the receiver, and sat with her head between her hands, her elbows on the desk. She had known, of course, had always known, that this moment must come. But now it had come and she must be ready to hear that he was no more. Should she go to him? How could she decide?

Would not her presence sharpen for him the agony of separation? Better to leave him with his children; better to let him slip away into the unknown with his children about his bed.

She rose, undecided, and finding house and gardens intolerable she got into her small convertible, which she always drove herself, leaving her larger car to her chauffeur, and alone she drove toward the sea. The coastline of Jersey was impossibly crowded and she drove northward toward Southampton. Somewhere beyond Red Hills she would, perhaps, find a lonely cliff by the sea and there imagine a spot where her house could stand apart. By midnight she could be back. Yet what was the haste? Death would not wait and she knew she could not go to Edwin to see him die.

. . . At sunset she found the spot for which she searched. Between two towns she found a cliff and upon the cliff an emptiness. Doubtless it belonged to the owner of some great estate, but she would persuade him to sell. It belonged to such a person for at one side of the cliff, almost hidden by overhanging trees, dwarfed by sea winds, she discovered a narrow stairway leading to a small white beach between rocks. The steps were not often used, for they were covered with fallen leaves and moss, but they could be used, although she resisted the idea of using them now, because she was alone and if she slipped there would be no one to discover her plight, and darkness was falling fast, for the days were growing shorter. She must go back.

. . . It was midnight before she reached home and Weston was waiting for her.

"The telephone, madame. You're to call, if you please, this number. And you had me worried, madame, if I may say so, you being alone like that and the night being black and no moon."

"Thank you, Weston," she said, moving to the telephone.

80

He bowed and went away and she rang and waited. In a moment the same voice answered, which this morning she had heard.

"Mrs. Chardman?"

"It is I."

"I've been waiting. My father died at six o'clock. His last moments were very painful. We were all about his bed. But the strangest change is taking place, a transfiguration. All the lines of pain are fading away. A beautiful peace—"

The voice broke.

"He was very beautiful," she said softly.

The voice began bravely. "Yes—much more beautiful than any of his children. The funeral will be on Thursday. Will you come?"

"No," she said quickly. "I don't want to think of him as dead. For me he lives—forever."

"Thank you," he said.

Silence then and she put up the receiver. That part of her life, that strange interlude which she could never explain to anyone, and would never, that, too, was over. She sat for minutes in remembering thought. Somehow she felt no bereavement. She would be forever grateful for what Edwin had given her. Into the void of her loneliness he had poured love, generous unselfish love, asking no return except her occasional presence. She was glad the love had been fruitful for him, too, inspiring him to a philosophical search which he might not otherwise have undertaken. She had brought him comfort.

She pulled out a drawer where she kept his letters, and choosing at random, she took up one which had come to her only last week.

"To me, about to die—perhaps before we meet again, my darling, though God forbid—it has become essential to define the problem of death before I can hope to solve it. Are those who have died ahead of me conscious of anything? For this answer I must wait.

81

Yet I dare hope, for else why should I feel in these days a curious readiness to die, amounting almost to a welcoming of death, as though I wished to rid myself of this body of mine, which has served its final purpose, my beloved, in our love. Without love I must have believed death final; with love, my hope becomes even more than faith. It becomes *belief*."

She let the letter fall from her hands. She lifted her head, she listened. The house was silent about her but in the silence she seemed to hear music, distant, undefined.

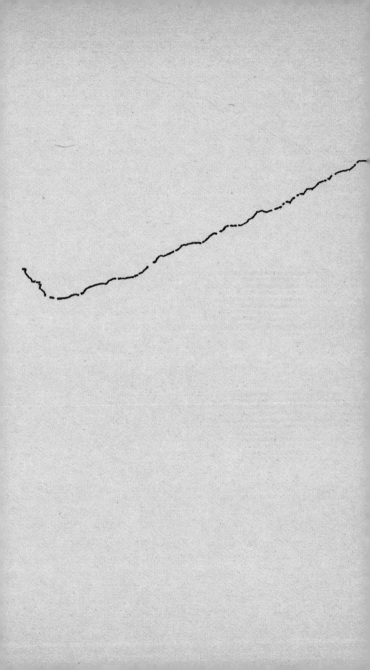

Part Two

"I SUPPOSE it began in Asia," Jared Barnow said, "or, pinpointing further, in South Vietnam, in that beastly little war concentrated there."

He had simply dropped in one evening in early autumn when, she thought, she had all but forgotten him in the absorption of the new house. She had chosen the land, twenty acres on a cliff, and had even picked the site for her house, among a cluster of wind-shaped cedars. She had driven home in a mood of contentment, if not of joy—for what had she to do with joy at this stage of her life?—and had found him waiting for her in the dusk on the terrace. He was pacing back and forth, impatient.

"No one knew where you were," he complained. "It's very unwise of you. Suppose something happened to you! Anything can happen these days. Where would I look for you?"

She smiled, telling him nothing. "I'll join you in a jiffy."

Half an hour later, she looked at him across the dinner table. Above the silver bowl of hothouse roses the candles flickered and Weston closed the French windows opening to the terrace and left the room.

"You've never told me about that part of your life," she said.

"No." He ate for a moment in silence, which she did not interrupt. Then he began again.

"I doubt I'll ever tell you. There are parts of one's life that must be closed, absolutely, except as they explain the present. I'll tell you—"

But he did not tell her and she did not inquire, speaking instead of small present events in her own life, a new sonata she had begun, her piano lessons with a celebrated teacher. Then abruptly when they were in the library for coffee—"Let's go to the library," he had said. "The drawing room terrifies me, somehow" —and when the door was shut and they were alone he began again.

"This much is necessary to tell, perhaps because it gave me my direction. There was a rocket attack on Saigon. The enemy aim was never accurate and one of the rockets fell on a village just outside the city where we were stationed. It wasn't a severe attack, it didn't last long, but the damned thing fell on a huddle of children who were scrambling in the dust for some chocolates one of our men had thrown down. They were laughing and shouting when"—he closed his eyes and bit his lower lip and then went on—"the man who had tossed the sweets was blown to bits. Most of the kids weren't so lucky. They were only wounded. We gathered the ones still alive and carried them to the makeshift hospital we'd set up in the village. There weren't enough doctors or nurses. There never were."

His hands trembled as he tried to light a cigarette and he gave it up. "There's no use going into all of it. But that day I stood by at a makeshift operating table, trying to help a surgeon who was removing bits of metal from a child's brain. I was horrified—and angry—to see the tools he was using: carpenter's tools on gossamer! The boy died. I was glad for that. What could life be for him? But somehow all my anger at what had happened—was happening—centered on that clumsy tool. At *least that* could be improved! So—

if you can imagine—out of fury, a dedication was born. I suppose one must call it dedication. It's a drive, a concentration, a crystallization of purpose in my field, which has always been science, but a practical science. I'm not purely a theorist. I like to see a theory put to use. My father was an engineer. I've inherited the instinct."

He rose abruptly from his chair and, walking to the closed window he stood, his back to her as though he were gazing at the garden, now dimly appearing in the moonlight, and he went on talking.

"It wasn't just the one child. Thousands! Even the Vietcong didn't use napalm. We did. But we weren't deliberately *personally* cruel as some of our own Vietnamese allies were. I saw a Vietnamese officer—there was a woman in a village just frozen in terror with two children clinging to her and another in her arms— shoot the children one after the other and then shoot her in the belly. Why? He was our ally—one of them. But it wasn't a matter of one or a thousand. The children could never run fast enough. Bombs, bullets, mines, poisoned bamboo spikes, artillery shells, napalm—the whole works. Not just children, either, but everything seemed to center in that little boy whose brain I saw as that wretched instrument—exposed it. I was about to be discharged. I'd served my time. A week later I was on my way home. But I've never forgotten."

She listened in silence as he revealed himself. He revealed himself and yet the revelation removed him infinitely far from her. She had lived her life in such safety, such peace, such remoteness from the world he had known that Edwin's death, and even Arnold's, dwindled now to mere incidents, inevitable and scarcely sorrowful. How could she comfort this young and stricken man? She felt a surge of helplessness, weakening in its power. She did not know what to say and so said nothing and felt the more helpless. Then suddenly he seemed to need no comfort. He turned resolutely and squared his shoulders.

"Why have I told you all that? I've never mentioned it before. I came home, I went to work. Who is to say that it was all meaningless? Pour me another cup of coffee, will you?"

He held out his cup and she filled it and he sat down again.

"So," she said, putting the silver coffee pot on its tray, "what are you working on now, specifically?"

He smiled at her gratefully over the edge of his cup and, setting it down empty, he began with his usual enthusiasm. "I'm not ready yet for specifics. Basically I'm a physicist. That's my training. I'd have proceeded in that field, remote from human lives, I suppose, and wandering further and further into nuclear physics, if I had not been thrown into Vietnam—from which I shall never extricate myself now, emotionally, at least. I have lost my interest in space. I'm earthbound. But if I'm to apply my physics, I need engineering, biomedical engineering."

He frowned absently as he paused. He had forgotten her, she perceived, half jealously, and she pondered in some secret recess of her mind whether she should recall him by a feminine trick, an exclamation, softly uttered, that he was getting beyond her comprehension. So might she have done had she not been the daughter of Raymond Mansfield, that eminent scientist, who had lived so entirely as a scientist that she, alone with him in this house after the too-early death of her mother, had absorbed not only understanding of his scientific jargon, but an actual comprehension of his work with cosmic rays, at least to the degree of being able to help him with measuring and testing instrumentation. The exactitude demanded by such scientific pursuits had bred exactitude in her being, expressed in honesty carried sometimes to an extreme.

This honesty prevented her now from a feminine

trick, and she merely said, rather quietly, "I understand. Of course, I haven't followed the developments in engineering, but I remember my father's impatience with his own imperfect instruments when he was measuring cosmic rays on mountaintops and in caves. He used to mutter to himself that goddamit why hadn't he taken a course in ordinary engineering!"

Jared laughed. "Exactly! Well, universities today are planning courses in biomedical engineering and I shall simply have to—"

He broke off.

She waited, and then asked in the quiet almost indifferent voice with which she had been speaking, "And how, exactly, do you define biomedical engineering?"

He looked at her surprised and then considering. "Well, it's an interdisciplinary sort of thing, as I think I've told you—multidisciplinary, if one is to be exact. For example, if I develop nuclear instrumentation—which I may decide upon—I must have electronic engineering for making my tools. But since I want to work in the medical field I must proceed further with biology."

"That makes you a physico-biological engineer?"

"Exactly."

He looked at her with suddenly quizzical eyes. "Strange talk, this, isn't it? Between a young man and a beautiful woman?"

"It brings back my talks with my father, when I was a girl," she said.

"You still don't look more than a girl," he said.

She felt his eyes upon her then and, looking up, met as surprised a gaze as though he saw her for the first time. Accustomed as she was to abrupt appreciation in a man's look, she was instantly absurdly shy. She had often been told that she was a beautiful woman, although she did not think herself beautiful, being too tall, she thought, and inclined to be too thin and perhaps too fair, not at all voluptuous looking or anything of that sort. So she had thought somewhat apologetically when she was Arnold's wife, yet here was the "look" again, as she called it to herself, a look unwelcome until now, when to her own surprise, it was not at all unpleasant. She met his dark eyes, not boldly in the least, but with a sort of pleading.

"I suppose it's because I'm too thin," she said, her voice so low as to sound breathless.

"You're exactly right," he replied firmly. "I'm glad you're tall and leggy. I like it."

She laughed, to evade this declaration. "What am I supposed to say now?"

"Whatever you feel," he directed promptly.

"Well, then, I'm pleased, though surprised."

"Come now—I don't believe you're surprised."

He gazed at her, daring her, and she felt her cheeks flush. She was about to protest her age in self-protection and then did not, discovering in herself a reluctance even to think of the difference in their ages. What did it matter if really it did not? They were two human beings who by accident had been born a generation apart. So it had been with herself and Edwin, only that was different, was it not, since he was the man?

"What are you thinking of?" Jared asked suddenly.

She laughed in embarrassment. "Has one person the right to ask that of another?"

"Meaning you won't tell me?"

"Meaning I won't tell you!"

They exchanged half-smiling, half-challenging looks and then she rose.

"Thank you for telling me about the child. I shan't forget. It explains so much. Do you mind if I say good night? I'm a little tired tonight."

. . . Safely in her own room and alone, she sat down before her dressing table and stared at herself in the oval, gilt-framed mirror that hung above it. What she saw was different, or so she imagined, from the woman she had looked at, without exactly seeing her, this morning when she was brushing her hair after her shower. This woman, reflecting herself now, looked, she decided, glowing—a ridiculous word. As though she were naïve enough to *glow,* if one must use the word, merely because a young man seemed inclined toward falling in love with an older woman who happened to be herself! Older she was, and she had all the sophistication, she believed, that a woman should have at her age.

Her acquaintance, if not her friendship, was wide, and she was quite accustomed to the attachments between men and women these days, old and young, young and old. For that matter, what about herself and Edwin? But could she ever have explained that relationship to Arnold? Perhaps life was merely a series of experiences that could not be explained even to one's self. And it was true that she now looked years younger than she was, which she had not before Arnold died, or indeed, even before Edwin died. Alone, she had in fact reverted to her own natural youthfulness, the effect, perhaps, of complete freedom, in which it was not necessary to share anything of herself, her time, her thoughts, with anyone else.

"And I shan't give up my precious freedom to anyone now," she said to the woman in the mirror. She smiled and the woman smiled back at her. Yes, she thought, taking the pins out of her hair, she had said goodnight to Jared Barnow at exactly the right moment. He possessed a powerful animal magnetism which she was too intelligent not to recognize. She was aware, too, of the possibility of response within herself. Beneath the fastidiousness of her taste, the restraints of her upbringing, she was strongly sexed, how strongly she did not know—did not, indeed, want to know. Such knowledge could be very upsetting, the consequences too serious to be worth the experience. She was not afraid of the judgments of other persons, for in these days of laxity and indulgence such judgments were so light as to cause little more than amusement, but she dreaded the consequences in herself. Knowing the intensity of her feelings, she knew also that if she allowed herself to consider an—attachment, call it, she might not be able to control it. Then again her new freedom would be lost.

She began to brush her hair vigorously and the long bright stuff fell over her face like a flimsy veil.

· · · "You have a strange effect on me," Jared announced at the breakfast table.

"Yes?" Her eyebrows lifted. She was quite herself this morning after a night's deep sleep, her mind relaxed after decision.

"A creative effect," he went on. "Instead of distracting me, as I've known myself to be distracted by an attractive woman, you—I hate to use the word inspire, it's so misused, but that's what it amounts to for me. You start my ideas into ferment. I've not met a woman before who appeals to every side of me—mentally, emotionally—and now, physically, too."

He spoke simply and without embarrassment, as he might have done had he been explaining a new theory. She listened, her eyes upon his, and answered as simply.

"That's wonderful to hear."

He waited, their eyes still meeting. "Well?" he said after a moment.

She smiled. "Well what?"

"Is that all?"

"What more can there be?"

"Any more, as much as you wish."

Silence fell, a portentous silence, swelling into an immense possibility. He was looking at her steadfastly— daring her perhaps? A word, a sign of yielding, and they might be thrown into a moment irretrievable in its implications. She was aware of his readiness, his hand waiting there on the edge of the table, his whole being waiting and ready. She withdrew involuntarily from the challenge.

"Let's talk about something else," she said.

He was silent then and fell to his eggs and bacon, until she broke the continuing silence, her voice casual. "Must you work today or have you time for a horse-back ride?"

"You ride?"

"I've taken it up again. I used to ride a great deal as a girl, but my husband didn't care for it."

"He didn't appreciate you." His voice was accusing, his mouth sulky.

"In his way he did—very much," she insisted.

"Then he didn't understand you."

She laughed. "Oh, come, that's too trite—husbands that don't understand wives, wives that don't understand husbands! You haven't told me about the girl who wants to marry you. Is she interested in your work?"

"She wouldn't know what I was talking about."

"You remind me of my son, Tony. He married a charming, stupid girl. And he's quite intelligent! I suggested that she was perhaps a little stupid—only I didn't use the word—when he told me he wanted to marry her, and he replied that he didn't want a damned intelligent woman to come home to at night."

She laughed once more but he did not laugh with her. He looked at her gravely, scrambled egg poised on his fork. "He's a damned fool, I'd say!"

"Oh, no, Tony's not a fool. Just had enough of his mother! I felt quite pleased—an only son not attached to his mother? That's success for the mother these days."

He ate the egg, reflecting. "I wish you wouldn't talk about husbands and wives, sons and mothers," he said peevishly.

"Only about you and the girl—" she said.

"Not even about her. All right, let's go riding now. I have an appointment this afternoon." He rose and pushed his chair in as he spoke.

... Riding, she thought remorsefully, was not a good idea after all. He rode superbly, his slender figure erect and elegant, the reins loose in his hand and yet controlled. Then there was the weather, a warm bright day, sunlight dappled through the trees on either side of the trail, the autumn-tinted hills rolling away to the horizon. She knew she looked well in her riding clothes and at the thought was severe with herself again. Had there been some secret impulse of coquetry which she had not recognized this morning at the breakfast table? No, she had simply been happy, a bright morning, a comfortable, even beautiful house, a pleasant companion. And surely there was no danger in admiring this companion, young and handsome, oh, very young and very handsome!

"Why are you smiling at me?" he demanded.

"Secret thought," she said. "Come, let's gallop!"

She touched her whip to her horse's flank and led the way down the trail and into the valley. And flying along under the cloudless sky, she thought of the house on the cliff, nonexistent and yet as real to her imagination as though it stood there. Should she tell him of that house? Yield to the impulse to reveal herself to him? No! The decision cut clean across the impulse. She would not reveal herself—not yet. She slowed her horse to a canter and glanced at her wristwatch.

"It's noon—you have an appointment."

"Why do you try to escape me?" he cried.

"Do I?" she asked, and then, avoiding his eyes, she touched the whip to her horse's flank and broke again into a gallop.

... "You do try to escape me, you know," he said an hour later. He had declined luncheon, declaring that he had no time and now he was taking his leave.

They stood at the door and he looked down into her upturned face.

She met his gaze frankly. "I don't try to escape you—it's just that I—"

She broke off, he waited.

"You'll be late," she said.

"I'll be late," he agreed, and waited.

"I don't know how to answer you," she said at last.

"Ah, that's better. So next time we'll find out why you can't answer me."

He stooped and kissed her mouth, very swiftly, very lightly, so that she could not step back or turn her head to avoid him. Then he was gone.

. . . He left an effect behind. She felt his absence so strongly that it became a presence. The silence in the house, his firm declarative voice no longer to be heard, his restlessness, moving from his chair, getting up to look out a window, to play for five minutes at the piano, to go to a bookshelf and pull out a book and glance through it while he talked and then put it back without speaking of it while he talked of something else—an infinite restlessness of the mind invading the body, his whole dominating, brilliant, demanding personality everywhere in the house, all this suddenly no more, was only an affirmation of himself.

She sat down when he was gone, her lips tingling with the kiss, and then as abruptly rose, refusing to recognize the surge of physical longing in her body. Let her recognize its meaning! There had been no great personal excitement in her life with Arnold, but there had been sexual content. He was not distasteful to her, and his approach was with a mature man's understanding of a wife's need. He had been considerate and appreciative, and she had been the same toward him, she believed. Certainly she did not want an extramarital love affair as so many women did nowadays, not merely on moral grounds but because she had no need

95

of it. Now let her face the fact that missing the regularity of her somewhat placid life with Arnold and perhaps even the stimulation of Edwin's touch, her natural desires, long awakened and customarily assuaged, were making demand upon her.

There was no need for shame or even embarrassment in this, a situation severely common enough, she reflected, when a wife lost her husband or a woman her lover. She had simply to face life as it was now and make her choices. She had chosen to live alone and explore her freedom. Therefore she must turn her mind, her imagination, away from Jared as a male. Let her put it as frankly as that, let her think of him as a human being, a friend and no more. Thus she admonished herself. Think no more of how he looks, she decided sternly; think instead of his mind, his interests, his career, all the aspects of his strong personality. There was no reason why she should not enjoy these, in freedom, instead of allowing an emotion to seize control of herself.

I shall prepare myself to be his friend, she thought, and remembering his admiration for her father, she slipped back into the days when she had been her father's daughter, the only one in his house who understood what he was talking about when he spoke of his work with cosmic rays, the only one who wanted to understand. And she had wanted to understand because she loved him and knew that, successful scientist that he was and famous everywhere in the world, he was lonely in his own house.

"Your mother is a darling good woman," he used to say to her, "and I've been a poor sort of husband to her, my mind always somewhere else, even when she's talking to me. It's no wonder she loses patience with me. I don't blame her a bit."

Her answer to this had been silence, then throwing her arms about him, then finally an endless patience with Arnold when he wanted to talk with her, though his work as a lawyer was monotonously dull, she thought, yet if she felt impatient, and she had, very often, she had only to remember her lonely father, and, yes, her impatient, lonely mother, filling her days with household detail, and her own impatience died. Yes, her father was lonely as only scientists can be lonely, working as they do and must with the vast concerns of the universe.

It occurred to her now that Jared, too, must be lonely, young though he was, but so much more brilliant than his fellows and living alone, too, with an old uncle. She could easily mend that loneliness and without thinking of it as a love affair, which indeed was the last experience she wanted. Once during her marriage she had been strongly attracted to a handsome man of her own age, a bitter time it had been, she hated the very memory of it, for the attraction had been purely physical, and she was thankful for that, for if she had been able to respect the man, she could not have resisted him. She had resisted, but she remembered and would always remember the frightening power of her own impulses, compelling her to yield herself until the impulse, resisted, became an actual pain, so intolerable that she had begged Arnold to take her to Europe that summer. Whether he knew why she had been so importunate she never knew and did not want to know even now. He had listened to her pleading, and had not asked why she was weeping while she talked, nor could she tell him why.

"Of course, my dear," he said. "I shall enjoy a vacation myself. There now—you're in a state of nerves —I've noticed it lately. You do too much—so many charities and so on and the children are at a trying age. I don't at all like the way Millicent answers you when you speak to her."

Millicent! That daughter of hers, now a complacent wife and mother, had she known why her mother had been so impatient and abstracted in those days? Had she perhaps ever seen them together, her mother and the extravagantly handsome man with blue eyes and dark hair silvered at the temples—a thin, aggressive, sharply pretty adolescent Millicent, critical with love for her father and jealous of her mother—

She put away such memories and thought of Jared in other terms. She would learn to know his mind, his thought, and in such ways assuage his loneliness, and her own need.

. . . "But you're looking so well," her daughter exclaimed.

"Should I not?" she inquired.

Millicent herself did not look well, she thought. The young woman had let herself gain weight, and her hair, dark as Arnold's had been, looked unbrushed, even unwashed, and she wore a dull blue suit that needed pressing.

"But you're rejuvenated," Millicent insisted so accusingly that her mother laughed.

"And is that sinful?"

They were in her upstairs sitting room, and here Millicent had found her not fifteen minutes ago. But it was her daughter's habit to let months pass without communication and then drop in upon her without warning.

"No," Millicent said reluctantly. "Not exactly," she added. She glanced at the papers on the desk where her mother sat, leaning forward and craning her neck to do so. "What are you drawing?"

"Plans for an imaginary house," she replied.

"House—that's what I've come about," Millicent exclaimed. "Your looking so blooming put me off. Tom wants a week's deer hunting in Vermont and I thought I'd go along with the children if you can lend us the house."

"Of course," she said. Then moved by a sudden and inexplicable impulse, she continued, "As a matter of fact, I'll give you the house, if you like."

98

"Why?" Millicent asked bluntly.

She hesitated. "I don't know exactly—except it's too lonely there for me."

"I can understand that," Millicent said. "There's no one in the world who could take Father's place."

"No. Nor would I wish it otherwise."

"Of course not."

They exchanged looks, hers smiling and a little sad, Millicent's almost curious. Then her daughter rose and, approaching, stooped to kiss her cheek. "I can't stay, Mother."

"You need a new suit," Edith said gently.

"Do I? Well, I won't get one! Tom's thinking of a new job. We'd have to move to San Francisco, though."

"Oh—so far?"

"It is far, but what can I do?"

"Go with him, of course—what else? But when?"

"That's the question. Tom said not to tell you until it's certain. But it slipped out."

"I'll keep it to myself. And what's distance nowadays? Or time?"

"True! Well, good-bye, Mother. Of course I'll see you before we go, if we go!"

They clasped hands and she clung to her daughter's hand.

"And if it's to be, when would it be?"

"We count on the end of the month, in time for Christmas in the new place."

Her daughter was gone, and she was alone again. Christmas? It meant then that the house would be empty. Tony's wife wanted their children to have Christmas in their own home. Arnold's death meant one change after another in her life. This old house remained as it was but everything in it was changed. It had really been his house, then! At least without him all its ways and habits were meaningless. If she continued to live here, she would live in a growing melancholy that in the end would stifle her. She took the receiver from the telephone desk.

"Is this the Wilton Real Estate office? Yes? Then may I speak to Robert Wilton, Senior? A few minutes? I'll wait—"

She waited until a hearty voice resounded at her ear.

"Yes, Mrs. Chardman! What can I do for you? Do you want to sell your house? I could make a fine sale for you if you—"

"Not yet, thanks! On the contrary, I want to buy."

"Well, now! You're moving?"

"There's a piece of land I want to own. Perhaps I'll put up a house of sorts, just for myself. It's by the sea—"

"Understandable, entirely understandable—a place by the sea. I seem to remember you always hankered—but I think Mr. Chardman didn't quite—still and all, there's no reason why you shouldn't have what you want now."

"None at all," she agreed.

"Where is this land?"

"It's in North Jersey, near a town but not in it. A part of a great estate, I think, on a cliff with surrounding forest. One passes several of those great old houses—"

She gave exact directions, and heard him breathing heavily as he took notes.

"What's your price range, Mrs. Chardman?" he asked.

"I just—want it," she said.

He laughed. "Then I suppose you must have it! Why not?"

"Why not?" she agreed again.

. . . The filmy flakes of an early snowfall were drifting through the morning air. The sky was gray, a November gray, that morning as she opened the heavy front door. Even the door seemed heavier than usual,

100

and she had more than once complained to Arnold about that door, hanging on immense brass hinges. Weston held the door open a moment now.

"I'm glad, madame, that you decided against driving yourself. It looks like a real snow—so quiet and all."

"Please tell Agnes not to disturb the papers on my desk upstairs when she is dusting."

"Yes, madame."

"I'll stop somewhere for luncheon but I should be home for dinner."

"Alone, madame?"

She hesitated. "I think I'll ask Miss Darwent to dine with me tonight."

She went to the telephone in the hall and dialed. "Amelia? Yes, it's Edith. I have an errand today in Jersey, but I'll be back in time for dinner. Will you dine with me? Eight o'clock—that gives me plenty of time. Oh, good—"

She hung up, and turned to Weston, patiently waiting. "She'll come, and she likes fresh losbter, remember!"

"Yes, madame."

She was off, then, and the heavy door shut behind her. The driveway made a circle and from the window of the car, through the drifting snow, she saw for an instant the formidable house of gray stone, standing like a German baronial castle in the midst of tall dark evergreens. Somehow she must escape that castle, but which way escape lay she did not know. And why was she pinning her faith on a house? The land was now about to be hers, however, the site, the place, the view over the ocean, the cliff, the small semicircular steps to the beach. Wilton Senior had accomplished that much. The estate was in the hands of heirs, and they had been eager to sell and, learning of this, she had offered to triple the acreage upon which she had first planned. She now owned sixty acres, far more than she needed, but they gave her room, and a wider view. She would let it grow wild. There would be no formal gardens, no cutting and clipping.

The morning slipped away in silence. The chauffeur drove smoothly and swiftly. Arnold had trained him to a controlled speed but she had increased the speed to the limit in recent months and without sign of protest or surprise he had accepted the change as though he understood why she wanted now to be driven faster. What he thought she did not know, a silent man, still young in her terms, at least—perhaps forty? She knew nothing about him and it never occurred to her to ask. Now, however, shut in by the snow, she felt the silence oppressive and broke it.

"William, are you married—children and so on?"

"No, ma'am. I live with my old mother."

"Old? How old?"

"Sixty-three, ma'am."

"In Philadelphia?"

"At present, ma'am. We used to live in North Jersey. My mother was housekeeper in one of them big old houses. That's how I know where to go now, ma'am. I grew up in those parts."

"Oh? And did you know the Medhursts?"

"Yes, ma'am. That's where my mother worked."

"How strange! I've bought some of the Medhurst land."

"So I've heard, ma'am."

She fell into surprised silence. Nothing in her life could be really private, she supposed, for Arnold had been well known in financial circles. But why should she care? She was herself the daughter of a famous man, the widow of a prosperous one. She had no need of secrets, and would have none, she decided firmly. To have no secrets was to be truly free. And so in this mood of freedom she arrived at her destination where she found Wilton Senior waiting in his car. He came to her at once.

"I brought the necessary papers for you to sign, Mrs.

Chardman. I think everything is in order, provided you're satisfied."

"Let me just look at my view and see if it is all I remembered."

The snow had momentarily ceased and she walked to the edge of the cliff and looked over the heaving gray sea. There was no wind to drive the waves to whitecaps, but far below her the surf broke heavily against the rocks that surrounded the beach. The chauffeur came to her side, also.

"I used to run down them steps, ma'am, when I was a kid, that is, and in the early morning before the family was up—all except Master Robert—Bob they called him. He wasn't so much older than me. There's good crabbing on that beach when the tide goes out."

"The steps don't look very safe now," she observed.

"No, ma'am. But I could put them into shape easily enough. I'm handy that way."

"Perhaps I'll ask you to do it for me."

"Yes, ma'am."

He went away when she said no more, and she continued to look out over the sea. Whether she ever built the house, this land was now hers. The house could be or could never be, but she stood firmly on her own land. The snow was beginning to fall again. She felt the flakes cold against her face, like the touch of cold fingertips, and she turned to Wilton Senior.

"I am ready to sign the papers," she said.

. . . "Whatever became of that house you were going to build?" Amelia inquired over the dinner table.

She had been absorbed in the lobster and until now she had asked no questions. Indeed, there had been no time, for Edith had been late. The snow had increased into a quiet storm, so that when Weston opened the heavy door it was to inform her immediately that Miss

Darwent had already arrived and was waiting in the library, the drawing room being too chilly for her, since the north wind had begun to blow on that side of the house.

"Tell her I'll be down in five minutes—I'll just change—and dinner can be served at once."

"Yes, madame." He hesitated and then went on, "I did tell the chauffeur when you were to be back, madame."

She paused at the foot of the stairs to smile, remembering the jealous hostility between these two faithful servants. "It wasn't his fault. The snow is already deep."

"Very well, madame."

In a few minutes she and Amelia were at the table in the dining room, where a fire blazed under the marble chimney piece. Amelia had drunk her clear soup promptly and was now busy with broiled lobster and melted butter, her napkin tucked into her collar.

"It's still only in the mind," Edith replied.

"You'll never find a more comfortable house than this," Amelia said. She was cracking a huge claw in a pair of pincers, and it gave way suddenly with a loud report.

"It will have a different sort of comfort," Edith said, and then smiling at her old friend, she went on, "If I had anything to tell you, I would tell you, Amelia. The truth is, I am in a curious state of mind, not confused really, but searching. I haven't quite found myself, I don't quite know what I want, or where it can be found. I'm just—enjoying life in a queer sort of way, perhaps not really facing anything—I don't know."

Amelia put down claw and pincers. "You're idle, that's what. You need something to do. Why don't you find a charity or something?"

"I don't want or need busy work," Edith replied. "I have my music—and books I haven't read and—"

"And what?" Amelia demanded when she paused.

"And friends. That's why I asked you to come here tonight. I haven't seen you—"

Amelia interrupted. "Who is that long-legged fellow who has been here a couple of times?"

"He's someone I happened to meet last winter in Vermont. He is an admirer of my father—"

"Not of you?"

"Oh, for heaven's sake, Amelia!"

"Well, you're ripe for it. I know—I've watched my friends when they've become widows after having faithful husbands like Arnold, especially pretty widows!"

"Please, Amelia!"

"Oh, very well, Edith! Don't tell me anything you don't want to tell me."

"Amelia, there's nothing to tell."

"Then why did you suddenly invite me to dinner?"

"Because I was lonely. I dreaded coming back to this great dark old house. And—and—"

"Be careful," Amelia said. "You're getting in the mood for anything. I'll have some more of the asparagus, Weston."

. . . "So why don't you come with me?" Jared asked.

His voice came clear and strong over the telephone. It was a crisp fine morning, the day before Christmas, and she had been wondering how she would spend the holiday. Millicent and her family had already moved to San Francisco, they had made telephone exchanges. The children were enchanted with the beautiful playgrounds, the beaches, the parks.

"And you?" Edith inquired.

"I'm going to have a maid," Millicent cried, "and of course I'm enchanted. Tom has a good raise."

"Then he's on his way up and all is well," she had said.

With this she had not forgotten her daughter exactly, but she was at ease about her and could forget her if she liked, very much as she habitually forgot Tony because really she was not needed any more, and so was free this morning to linger over breakfast, answer the telephone when it rang, and hear Jared's clear voice at her ear. She gazed out the wide French windows meanwhile. The sky was cloudlessly blue, but the last leaves were fluttering down from the big oak tree by the east terrace. She had finished breakfast, and was deciding what to do with the day, something vigorous, she had thought, for she was feeling unusually well, and awake, impatient for physical exercise, perhaps a canter alone along the edge of the woods.

"But when?" she asked, uncertain.

"I'll pick you up this afternoon and we'll motor down the eastern coast. Have pity on me. My old uncle is in the Virgin Islands—he hates the cold. And I can't think of anyone I'd rather spend Christmas with than you."

"You don't want to go to Vermont?"

"No. I want to take you to strange places where neither of us has ever been. Let's just wander."

She considered for a moment. On the inside pane of the wide window a late bee buzzed frantically, lost from its fellows, and she let herself be diverted.

"There's a bee buzzing on the window. If I let it out will it freeze?"

"No," he said. "It will find its way home."

"Then wait a minute," she said.

She opened the window and brushed the bee outdoors with her handkerchief. It flew away instantly, but the cold sweet air rushed into the room and she let it blow upon her face. The sharp chill stung her flesh and stirred her blood, she had not realized how close the air in this old house was, a scent not unpleasant, of leatherbound books and many Oriental rugs and hothouse flowers. A rush of impetuous desire for fresh-

106

ness and new vigor swept over her and she closed the window.

"I'll be ready," she called into the telephone.

"Good—at half past two," he said.

. . . The road wound in and out along the coast. For miles the sea was hidden, the road entering the forest and then as suddenly emerging again to the curve of a bay or a beach. The sun slipped slowly downward in the western sky and they stopped at twilight at an inn, an old mansion, its pillared portico reaching to the roof. Jared pulled up at the entrance.

"We've been very quiet," he said.

"Yes," she replied.

Neither of them had felt like talking, it seemed. He had driven the small convertible in concentrated thought and she had not interrupted. A few times he had noticed the landscape.

"Those rocks down there by the sea—" he said.

"As though they had been tumbled there by a giant—" she replied.

The air had been golden with sunlight through the afternoon, turning at sunset to rose and crimson. Evening star and a crescent moon hung over the trees and a beneficent calm pervaded her—and him, too, she felt, a relaxed mood which was in itself communication between them. She was happy in his presence, she now realized, happier than she had been for a long time, happier perhaps than she had ever been. Certainly with no one had she felt this conviction of life and its goodness, this ease of presence with another human being. She turned to him impulsively and found him looking at her, dark eyes questioning.

"Shall we stop here? Dine and then walk on the beach?"

"Yes," she said. "In this air—what is that scent? Pines, I think. It is too late in the year for flowers, though it's still warm in this climate."

"Pines warmed by the day's sun," he said. "And

shall we stay here for the night? At this season the inn will be nearly empty, I daresay—people at home for Christmas, but you and I are making our own Christmas."

"Let us stay," she said.

He gave her a look, passionate and deep, and for an instant she wondered what it meant. There could be no question, surely there could be no question about rooms, separate rooms. She was startled to discover in herself the question answered, hidden in her own being a reluctant yearning to forget her years and her reserves. She was no longer any man's wife. She was free to be what she wished to be, to do what she wanted to do. There was no need to refuse herself—or him—anything that pleased them. She had fulfilled all duties to others.

"Then I will engage our rooms," he said.

He left her in the car while he entered the office of the inn and she sat alone, a sweet intoxication pervading her. She recognized it without ever having felt it before, a powerful attraction to this man, an attraction of mind first, but so complete that it flowed through her body in a warm current. She tried to stay it, to control it, to analyze it. Let her remember herself. Let her ask herself what she truly wanted—no complications, she told herself, no foolish complications of emotion. Above all, no heartbreak at this time of her life.

He came back in a moment, very cheerful, very composed.

"I got adjoining rooms," he said. "If you want anything you can call me."

. . . She woke in the night as usual after five hours of sleep. That was her habit—five hours of deep dreamless sleep and then she woke absolutely, her mind clear and aware. Moonlight streamed through the open window and the air was crisply chill. She pulled the covers

108

about her shoulders and breathed deeply. There was a smell of the sea, the softly rushing sound of distant surf. This was how it would be in her house on the cliff when she slept there alone. Only now she was not alone. That is to say, Jared was on the other side of the closed door, not locked, only closed. She was suddenly acutely aware that it was not locked, only closed.

"There's no telephone between rooms in an old inn like this," Jared had said. "I'll not lock the door in case of—anything."

She had not replied. Instead she had stood quite still in the center of this big square room with its four-poster double bed.

"I hate to say good night," Jared said.

"It was a delightful dinner," she said. "I didn't know how hungry I was."

"Oh, I'm always a hungry beast." He twisted his handsome mouth in a wry smile as he spoke.

"You should be to cover that big skeleton of yours," she said.

He had not replied to this. Instead, after an instant of looking at her intently, he had put his arms about her and kissed her full on her lips.

"Good night, you darling," he said, and opening the door between the rooms, he closed it firmly.

. . . Now, lying in the big bed, she thought of the kiss. He had simply given it, taken it, without asking and without comment. She felt again the young warmth of his lips against hers as she remembered the moment. But was she not being ridiculous? What was a kiss nowadays? Women kissed men, men kissed women, with no feeling beyond a cheerful friendliness. Ah, but not she! She had never been one to give kisses easily or to welcome them. Even with Arnold they had seemed— unnecessary. As for Edwin, his kisses had been those of a child—or an old, old man, tender but pure. So what had this kiss been, this kiss which she still felt upon her lips? Then she rebuked herself again. The truth was that no one kissed her nowadays and she kissed no one. This one kiss lingered in her memory now merely because it was unaccustomed.

Then at this moment, as though to refute this self-deception, her body rose to defy her. She was suddenly seized by a surge of physical longing such as she had not known for years. No, let her be honest with herself. She had never known such longing, perhaps because she had always before this had the means of satisfaction. Now a door stood between and it was only closed, not locked. Suppose the impossible, suppose she got up from this alien bed, suppose she wrapped her rose silk negligée about her—it lay there on the chair—and suppose that she opened the door softly into that other room and then went in, even if it were only to stand and look at him as he slept. And if he woke and saw her standing there—

No, it could not be done. Perhaps, if she could be sure that he would not wake? But how could that be sure? And suppose his eyes opened, how could she know what she would see there? She did not know him well enough. She could not risk the possible rejection. She was too proud. Of course there were women who could cast away all pride, women who would count on physical response whatever the cost, but she knew herself. She could not escape herself, shamed. She would walk in shame, thereafter, and then whom would she have? She had only herself.

She lay rigid with desire, refusing to move, refusing to rise, refusing to walk across the floor, refusing the very imagination of what it would be to open the door and see him lying there, even sleeping. She forbade it to herself, until at last the throbbing of her body subsided and she slept.

. . . In the morning when she woke the memory of the night remained vividly with her, nevertheless. She lay remembering, and she listened. He was already up. Through the thin wooden door she could hear him moving about, and she listened for a moment and then got out of her bed and turned on the shower and dressed, putting on another suit than the one she had worn yesterday with her sable jacket. She wanted to be beautiful today, really beautiful, and aware that she was changeful in her looks, sometimes looking almost plain, she took pains with every detail. Ah, but she had not cared until now! Amelia was disgustingly right. Though she had no lover, yet the possibility of love produced a new vitality, stemming from the enlivened heart, the quickened bloodstream. Life became worth living again. The experience of the night had changed him for her, and she knew now she could love him. Yet she would not let herself say, even in the silence of her heart, that already she loved him. She was too sophisticated for that. She did not know him well enough, and might never know him well enough, for the completeness and the complexity of the true meaning of love, a word she never allowed herself to use as she daily heard it used, carelessly, and in regard to a multiplicity of objects and persons, expressing mere fondness or exaggerated liking.

No, she recognized the longing of last night for what it was, a yearning in her loneliness for a companionship most easily and simply expressed through a shared physical experience. She was grateful that she had forbidden herself. Nothing could be less gratifying to her than such an experience, prematurely expressed, so that afterward their relationship would have come to an abrupt end.

Their relationship—what was it? She asked herself the question and her only answer was another question. What could their relationship be, accepting as they must the difference in their ages? Let her crucify herself upon that fact! Yet had she not been even younger than some of Edwin's children? Ah, but he was a venerable man, a philosopher, dreaming of love as a philosophy, the shadow of himself as he lay beside her, a white ghost in the night. She had loved him for his beauty but her love had not been impelled by longing. She gave it gladly because he deserved every gift she could give, and this for no other reason except that he was worthy. Nor had she now any regret whatsoever.

Arnold of course would never have understood, nor, she guessed, could Jared, if he ever knew. For that matter, she herself did not understand. Probably her nature being human and no less selfish than that of other persons, she needed the comfort of Edwin's adoration. Perhaps that was all it was, an inglorious need, just as for years she had accepted Arnold's faithful love as her husband, returning what she could of her own love as his wife, which was, nevertheless, as she very well knew, much less in measure than his.

It occurred to her later, as she sat facing Jared at the breakfast table, that she was in grave danger of loving him as she had never before loved anyone. The morning sun shone full on him, she having chosen to sit with her back to the window, and thus she saw all too delightfully well his clear dark eyes, the firm line of his brow, his straight nose and beautifully sculptured mouth, all details of a totally unnecessary beauty. He was lit with a morning joy, ready to laugh, hungry for food and eager for pleasure—and innocent, she thought, touchingly innocent, at least so far as she was concerned. She rubbed salt relentlessly into the wound of this conviction.

"Tell me," she said, "how it is that you are not with that pretty girl of yours?"

He was eating scrambled eggs assiduously.

"She is pretty," he said, "but she has a handicap—a huge noisy father. He's divorced and married again. I wouldn't mind his noise, if it were occasionally a little more than that, but it isn't. Just noise—noise—noise."

"Come now," she said laughing. "Define this noise."

"Well, hail-fellow-well-met, back-slapping, h'are ya, Jared, old boy stuff!"

"How did she come to have such a father?"

"She's not like that, at all, herself."

"No? What is she like?"

"Rather tall, but not very. Quiet. I think perhaps she's stubborn, or perhaps only pertinacious. Or again, maybe she's not quiet except when she's with me and she thinks that's the way I like her to be."

"Why not just encourage her to be herself?"

"Well, you see, as I said, I don't know what that is. Did I ever tell you that I love your hands?"

"No. What makes you think of them at this instant?"

"I'm looking at them—that's why. They're *telling* hands."

She gazed down at her ringless hands. "What does that mean?"

"They tell me what you are."

She resisted the impulse to ask what that was. Instead she pressed the crown of thorns upon her head.

"If you know hands so well, why can't you tell what your girl is like?"

"Oh, *her* hands!" He laughed shortly and then was suddenly grave. "I wish you wouldn't call her my girl. She's—well, not *that,* anyway."

"But?"

"I don't know. It's a problem."

"She is?"

"No. I am. Perhaps I shouldn't marry. I'm too involved in this work I've chosen. Even now, sitting here opposite you on this glorious morning, with a whole glorious day ahead of us, I am thinking about something I'm trying to do—to create, that is. It's an artificial hand, a great improvement over anything we have now. Perhaps I was looking at your hands without

113

knowing why I did, exactly. A man such as I am—I'm always at my work. It's in me, the inventing, the planning. Take the hand, for instance—"

He held up his own right hand, spare and shapely. "The saddest thing about someone's losing a hand is that the feeling power is gone. A hand is not only an implement, it's a sense organ. It's the eye of a blind man, it's the tongue of those who cannot speak. I am working on an artificial hand which is so articulated that it can almost feel. Surgeons tell amputees that artificial hands can work for them but they can't feel. Well, I'm about to make one that *does* feel—at least it feels shapes and maybe even textures. There'll be feeling fingers instead of a hook or a claw. Think of touching a woman's cheek with a hook or a claw—or think of never being able to feel a woman's cheek at all!"

"You are an artist," she said. "But then all scientists are artists, my father used to say. You think like an artist, at any rate, and I can see that you want what you create to be a work of art."

He put down his knife and fork, and beckoned the waiter.

"Coffee again, please, and get the check ready. And you're very intuitive, Edith! I want to see something that I can see only half blindly, as a musician goes about creating a symphony. He hasn't any idea of how to do it, but he blunders along, inventing as he goes. That's me, too. It's only the artist in a human being that makes him creative. Without it he's no more than a technician. God, but it's fun to talk to you! I hope you don't mind my calling you Edith? It's a beautiful name and it suits you perfectly."

"If you like it, use it," she said.

"I am Jared, of course."

"Yes, thank you."

"I should have thought of it before, but we've been close even without names. I often wonder why I am so

114

close to you—I've never had this feeling before, not with anyone. But the minute I saw you—remember that snowy night? You opened the door of your Vermont house to me and I was startled because I felt I'd found someone I'd been looking for, though I hadn't been conscious of looking for anyone. At that moment I knew that somehow—I didn't know how and I still don't know—my life would be linked with yours as long as we live."

She heard these grave words with dread and exultation. For he spoke them gravely, his voice earnest, his eyes gazing steadfastly into hers, and she received them as gravely. This was not the light speech of a playful young man to an older woman. He was not such a young man. Lighthearted and whimsical as he could be at times, he was profoundly serious as she had already perceived, weighted she sometimes felt by the very magnitude of his talents. She had never known so talented a human being, she herself talented enough to recognize the effect of overburdening talent. Some of her own loneliness through the years, she had suspected, came from her recognition that neither of her children had inherited the brilliance of her father's gifts. Accustomed as she had become to his special affection throughout her childhood and youth, she sometimes felt, half guiltily, that this had made Arnold and the children she had had by him dull by comparison. For this guilt she had tried to atone by meticulous attention to what she had considered duty. Now there was no longer need to think of duty and in the delight of this new relationship she recaptured, too, some of the joy of her youth. Concepts, ideas, words that she had not used except with her father flowed now from the storage of her memory, waiting to be spoken when needed.

Through the long sunlit morning such thoughts came and went through her mind but she did not speak them. Indeed as the miles sped by neither of them spoke. He drove expertly, but he was far away in some distant space of his own, and she, recognizing such absence, for her father had habitually slipped away into similar abstraction, sat in silence and relaxed happiness. The landscape was mild and without snow, the rounded hills and shallow valleys were still tinged with green, the people were amiable and unhurried. There was little sign even of Christmas. So quiet was the day that the quietude invaded her own being until she wondered if she had dreamed her passion of the night before.

. . . "I don't understand the nature of love," he said.

It was such a Christmas Day as she had never had. They stopped at noon near a small town, a mere village whose name she did not know, and took their Christmas dinner in a restaurant that was the only one open. The proprietor was an old man, without family, he told them, else he would have been in his own home.

"Buried my wife ten years ago," he said cheerfully.

Now, the meal over, they walked along the beach and Jared, out of unusual lightheartedness and chaffing, had suddenly become serious and declared that he did not understand the nature of love. She leaned against the twisted weather-beaten trunk of a dead pine and waited for further communication. He stood beside her, looking out to sea. The day was quiet and the sea was still, but the first ripples of the incoming tide fringed the shore with white. He continued.

"What I really mean to say is that I don't understand my own state of mind."

She waited, having learned that though he was articulate enough when he spoke of his work, he was not at all articulate about himself, not because he was shy, she perceived, but because he was not accustomed to thinking about himself.

116

"For example," he went on, "when I am with you I am in the most curious contentment. I can't call it anything else—contentment. I feel I am somehow in my element. You make no demands on me. Do you realize, I wonder, how unusual it is for a woman to make no demands on a man? I don't have to charm you!"

She laughed. "I find you charming exactly as you are!"

He did not laugh in reply. Instead he continued to speak in the same half-musing mood. "No, I've never felt like this toward any woman. I have a sense of homecoming, of there being no need for secrets between us."

"Have you secrets?"

"Of course! A man of my age with no secrets? Impossible—in this day, anyway! I've played the fool as much as any man. My uncle—bless his reticences— could never bring himself to give me any advice and I stumbled along on my own, always too old for myself, always ahead of my own years. Yet I don't understand the nature of love." He turned to face her. "Mind you, I'm no innocent. I'm precocious in everything. A woman initiated me when I was thirteen. . . . Well, I let myself be initiated!"

"Don't tell me about it," she said quickly.

"I *will* tell you," he insisted. "I was in school—prep school—and one of the masters had an ardent wife. He was a chilly sort of fellow and she was a redhead, with all that goes with the temperament. She—well, it was a rape, I suppose, except that I was infatuated and big for my age—and once the final moment began, I couldn't stop. There's a point which, if a man lets it get that far, there is simply no stopping, and physically I was a man. It happened in her own house, too, on a rainy afternoon. I'd gone over to ask my professor a question in physics. I was doing advanced work and so I was a sort of favorite of his. I know now, of course, that he had a homosexual bent, which explained her, I suppose. But after she initiated me into the way of the flesh, so to speak, I simply became obsessed, to put it bluntly. I thought about nothing but sex. Are you shocked?"

"No," she said quietly, "only terribly sorry for that boy."

He did not reply to this, but continued his story, almost coldly, she thought. "It didn't matter how many experiences I had or with whom. They all ended the same way—in a sort of disgust with the woman and with myself. I couldn't understand why. She—whichever she happened to be—was always irresistibly attractive until I'd slept with her—maybe not at once but inevitably, and then it would be over. I'd stop seeing her then. I suppose I knew subconsciously that there was no real relationship there—a blind demand of the body, meaningless so far as communication went, like eating when you're hungry. Anyway, slowly, I grew beyond the meaningless stage. I simply stopped. I saw that I was destroying something in myself. I was destroying the capacity to communicate on any other level than sex. As soon as I'd got to like a girl—or a woman—and that might happen instantaneously, I thought of her physically. What confuses me more is that I think of you in the same way except it is entirely different with you—it's on every level at once."

She did not speak, could not speak, so confounded was she by her own feelings, a mixture of relief and quick hurt. A moment passed and she perceived that the insistent foolish hurt prevailed. Yes, she was hurt, her vanity as a woman, she told herself harshly, and she maintained steadfast silence. Not for anything would she reveal this self to him.

"Instead," he was saying, "I am conscious in your presence of a beautiful freedom to be myself, to think my own thoughts, plan my work, consider the future—in short, to *live,* and more freely even than when I am alone, because you broaden my freedom just by being the person you are, instead of making demands, limiting freedom as other women do. I'm hopelessly in love with you, I suppose, but not as I've been before. So I say that I don't understand the nature of love. I only know that I love you—in a way that is entirely new to me. I don't think I'll ever love anyone else." He turned to her abruptly and putting his hands on her shoulders, he looked into her eyes. "What do you say to all this?"

She shook her head. What could she say? Something banal, perhaps. I'm old enough to be your mother, you know. No, she could not. Her own heart refused the words. She had no feeling of a mother toward him. She had no wish, no will, to play the mother to him and she would not use a lie to cover the truth, that she loved him passionately.

"Well?" he demanded.

"I don't understand our relationship, either," she said at last.

He turned his eyes from her then, but he did not move away from her. Instead he put his arm about her shoulders and they stood thus, side by side and facing the sea until she was able no longer to endure the pressure of his body against hers. She moved from him.

"Let's get on our way, shall we?" she said.

"Where to?" he asked.

"Anywhere," she said.

. . . "And so," Jared was saying, "I want to devise an instrument that a cineplastic surgeon can use to create two fingers out of a forearm to substitute for the lost hand. I know how to do it, I think and, with training, the amputee will be able even to *feel* in those fingers. That's always my purpose, to restore the sense of feeling. But it's still the brain that interests me most. No one really understands the structure of the human brain. There the source of feeling is lodged—feeling and emotion and thought, of course. I'm studying the biology of the brain, dissecting a brain, actually, in my laboratory, so that I can devise certain instruments—ah, there's so much to do!

"The ordinary stethoscope, for instance, needs radical improvement. I want to study it, too, in depth; in spite of its general use and acceptance, I've an idea it needs a thorough revaluation, though new models keep appearing. There's been no basic acoustical study of it for years. There must be something wrong, or lacking, in it or there wouldn't be such an evidence of need for improvement. There ought to be a total soundway, for example, from the patient's chest to the listener's ear, excluding thereby all environmental noises. The three different wave forms—but why do I bore you with all this? You see what I mean—when I am with you my mind runs on its own way, only with more than normal creative energy, as though your presence provides an environment of conducive waves. Why not? There's physiological evidence of that sort of thing. We don't half understand the electrical effect of one personality on another."

She listened to this monologue and at the pause she replied with literal understanding. "Entirely possible, of course—and probable. And I love the way your mind ferrets here and there and everywhere, like an inquisitive animal quite apart from the rest of you. Sometime, of course, you'll have to exert the disciplines of the artist as well as of the scientist, both of which you are, and then you'll have to choose where to concentrate your direction. Oh, yes, you are an artist"—for he was shaking his head—"I've seen what you draw on bits of paper when you're thinking out one of your inventions!"

It was quite true. In the room in the Vermont house she had found scraps of paper on the desk whereon he had drawn sketches of animals, of human faces—one of these her own—and of intricate geometric designs. In the guest room in the huge old Philadelphia house she had discovered other such drawings and had carefully preserved them all.

"Not that I belittle inventions," she went on, "but inventions are never permanent. Someone else always thinks of an improvement and the invention on which a man has spent, perhaps, his life, is outdated. But art is eternal, ageless, complete in itself."

He cried out his admiration. "God, how accurately you put it! Entirely true, of course, and I shan't forget. But you know what you've done? Suddenly what I thought was to be my lifework, you've made into an avocation. I shall have to reconsider."

His handsome face fell into grim lines, his mouth grew stern, he muttered to himself unintelligible sounds. She perceived that she was forgotten and was well content.

. . . That night, on the way home and stopping at the same inn, he took her in his arms before they parted, and holding her against him, he kissed her, drew back to gaze intensely into her eyes, then kissed her again and yet again before he let her go and turned toward his room. She closed the door between them, giving him a last smile as she did so, but he opened it again to thrust head and shoulders through the opening.

"That smile—" he began abruptly and stopped.

She was already standing before the mirror, taking the hairpins out of her hair and she looked over her shoulder at him.

"Did I smile?" she asked.

"You did—a damned Mona Lisa sort of smile it was, too," he retorted, and closed the door without further comment.

She stood motionless before the mirror, and saw herself reflected there, not smiling at all but serious, her face flushing, her eyes too bright. A moment had arrived, a moment of decision. If she should open the door and simply enter his room without a word the moment would be hers, the wound would be healed, her own demand satisfied. For in truth how little he understood her! She made immense demand upon him, the final demand. "With my body I thee worship!" Was she afraid of refusal? Not at all—not at all! Alone with him in unknown country, in a half-empty inn, the night concealing all, he could not resist her. That he was not virgin, that he had spoken so freely of himself, only deepened her own desire. She would not be violating a boy. She would be offering her love to a man. For now she had rejected utterly the word infatuation. She loved him. Unwise, incredible, indeed reluctant, she was now irretrievably in love—not with a girl's shallow emotion, but with a woman's depth and power.

She took two steps toward the door and paused. Then resolutely she turned back again to the mirror and continued to take the pins out of her hair until it fell about her shoulders, a shimmering mass, out of which her face appeared, pale and of a startling beauty.

. . . "I have a bone to pick with you, in fact, several bones."

Thus he began the next day as soon as they met face to face at the breakfast table in the nearly empty dining room of the inn.

"Bone by bone, one at a time, please," she begged, as he pushed in her chair.

She was conscious of a deep weariness this morning, for she had not slept well. Broken dreams, always ending in frustration of some sort, a wandering road she walked alone, which ended suddenly without reason, a river in which she swam, unable to reach a shore, a crying child whom she searched for and could not find—from such dreams she had waked this morning, listless and without her usual morning energy.

"First, an exception to your saying that the inventions of science outdate themselves. Mathematics never does! All mathematics, if correctly done, are true. New discoveries may demand new equations, but the mathematics remain true, *if* correct. There's something eternal about mathematics. Who was it—someone—said that mathematics is the music of logical thinking and of course music is the mathematics of art?"

He sat down as he poured this forth, and she put up her hands in laughing protest.

"Wait—wait! It's so early in the morning—"

Was this what he had been thinking about in the night while she was weaving her futile dreams?

"I'm sorry," he said penitently. "But you've spoiled me, you know. I've grown used to simply beginning where I am, when I'm with you. I couldn't sleep last night for some reason. I'd half a mind to wake you up, too, but it would have been too selfish of me, though I'm selfish enough, God knows, so I lay thinking about what you'd said and trying to justify myself in my choice of work by reasoning out the relationship between science and art—which this morning seems to me to be that art concerns itself with beauty and science concerns itself with reality. Perhaps we couldn't face the harsh reality without seeing the beauty, too. We need both science and art."

"In the same person?" she asked.

"If the person is big enough," he said firmly. "And do you want your eggs scrambled this morning?"

"Yes, please," she said.

. . . The verbal duet continued later in the day, in the unplanned give and take which she was beginning to enjoy so keenly. This slipping in and out between the ephemeral of everyday incident and eternal verities was something she had not known before. She had listened to her father and to Edwin, obedient to their age and wisdom, but keeping her thoughts and arguments to herself. Now and again during her life as a student and then a wife, she had met brilliant men at a dinner table, at an evening's entertainment, and had even become absorbed for a time thereafter in their dominating brilliance, but she had not met a man, a young man, fearless as Jared was fearless, in his instinctive recognition of her as a woman but his equal, indeed at times his superior, which instead of an invitation he seemed to consider a delight. Such acceptance was new to her.

The morning passed in amiable conversation between long pauses of silence as he drove and she contemplated the changing landscape. It was noon, after an unusually long silence, that he suddenly spoke and the duet began again.

"I don't understand the creative process, whether in science or art. I know the process, of course—a long time, hours or days or weeks, when I simply muddle along in a morass of confusion. My mind is like a frantic animal locked in a cage, racing this way and that, searching for a door. Then suddenly the door is there. But it wasn't there all along. It appears without cause and without reason, and I am inspired."

"Because you've been searching," she said. "You've created your own inspiration because of your own demand—I suppose upon your subconscious. That's where the mind goes for its sources. It's the reservoir each of us has, perhaps the only one. That's what makes great art—the artist draws upon the reservoir. Otherwise how understand abstract art? It's successful only when it truly expresses that in the subconscious which is common to us all."

"How is it you know so much?" he demanded.

She still refused to allow herself to speak of her age. Call it vanity, but there were ways in which she was indeed vain! She equivocated.

"I had intelligent parents," she said.

"It's odd, but I don't want to know anything about your husband—or your children."

"They wouldn't understand you," she said quietly.

"Then I don't have to understand them, do I?"

"No."

Her answer was literal. She would never try to explain the inexplicable fact of her relationship to him. She owed no one such explanation. She was alone, she was free.

. . . "I have been hearing the oddest gossip about you," Amelia said the next day.

Amelia had come for one of her infrequent visits, a morning call, made usually on her way from the hairdresser in the center of the city.

"Have you indeed," she murmured in pretended indifference.

She had reached home the night after Christmas and Jared had left her at once, as soon as he had seen her safely into the house.

"The best, the happiest Christmas I've ever had," he told her.

To take her in his arms when he parted from her was now his habit, so much so indeed that she wondered if it meant anything to him, after all. Certainly it meant too much to her, for her own peace.

"I'll be back on New Year's Eve," he said at the door.

She had closed it behind him and felt the house empty about her, a shell without life. She was glad to see Weston appear at the end of the hall, obviously waked out of sleep.

"If you'd told me you was coming, madame," he murmured reproachfully, taking her bags.

"I didn't know myself," she said and went upstairs.

Alone in her sitting room she had not gone immediately to bed. Instead she had lit the fire, always laid ready, had sat in the easy chair before it, reliving the past days and facing herself. I shall have to come to some sort of conclusion, she thought. I cannot go on as I am. It is too difficult. I must part from him or—she could not finish. Instead, a thousand memories of him flowed over her, the changeful expressions of his vivid face, his dark eyes now musing, now questioning, his mouth, his voice, the way his hair grew upon the back of his neck, his strong firm hands. She went to bed distraught with longing and waked this morning unassuaged, to face Amelia.

"I have indeed," Amelia said with affectionate mockery. "And not only hearing! I had a letter from Millicent out in California. She'd had a letter from Tony. Would you like to read her letter? I have it in my bag."

"No, thank you. If Millicent wants me to know what she thinks, she will write to me herself."

Amelia closed the handbag she had opened. "She asks me to find out what is going on, but not to trouble you or worry you. But you know me, Edith. I can't beat around bushes—never have, especially with you."

"So what did you reply to Millicent?" she asked, evading the bushes.

"I told her that whatever you did was your own business, but if the gossip was true, I thought you were not only lucky but damnably clever and every woman of your age would envy you. After all, Queen Victoria is dead and we've buried the Puritans and why should teen-agers have all the fun nowadays?"

They were sitting on the glassed porch, the sun streaming through the eastern windows. The gardener had filled the place with blooming poinsettias for Christmas and in the midst of warmth and light and color it was impossible to be anything but gay.

"Thank you, Amelia," she said.

She met her friend's inquisitive look with daring and determination. No, she would not tell Amelia about Jared.

"Is that all?" Amelia asked.

"That's all," she said.

"Then there's no truth to the gossip?"

"There's never truth to gossip."

"Have it your own way, my dear," Amelia said, getting to her feet.

"I intend to," she said and followed her friend to the door.

. . . Purposely during the week she reconstructed her usual life. She sat on three boards, of each of which she was a member, she consulted with her attorney over income tax matters in relation to Arnold's will, she bought herself a sealskin jacket and small hat to match, she opened her belated Christmas presents and wrote notes of thanks. The household moved in its usual ways, surrounding her with care and comfort, and she slept well at night, postponing decision. After all, she told herself, she had not been asked to make a decision. It was possible, perhaps, and why not, simply to go on as she was, welcoming Jared when he came to visit her, accepting this remarkable friendship as a friendship and nothing more.

In this frame of mind two days before New Year's, she gave directions after breakfast.

"Weston, Mr. Barnow will spend the next few days here."

"Very well, madame. Shall he be here for dinner?"

"Yes. Please tell cook to begin with fresh oysters. He is fond of them."

"Yes, madame."

She went into the greenhouse that opened from the dining room and cut yellow snapdragons and pink carnations which she arranged for the guest room. When this was done she stood, looking about her and imagining him here, asleep in the great old-fashioned bed, or reading in the sitting room of the guest suite. She was in a tranquil mood and at this moment she thought of him with tenderness rather than desire, although she knew that desire waited. She realized, too, his lone-liness, not only that he had no family except an old uncle, but the far deeper loneliness of the superior mind, dwelling in distant regions too far beyond the minds of others for ordinary companionship. She had seen her father's loneliness, had indeed known some-thing of the same loneliness in herself. Few women read the books that she read, or thought such thoughts as hers. Yes, she was quite right in clinging to this friendship. They were two people who communicated, in spite of the difference in their ages. Perhaps this very difference was her protection; if so, let it never be forgotten! Upon this she put away from herself every-thing except her joy, surely innocent, in his return.

. . . "Do you mind if I bring someone with me tomorrow?"

His voice, resounding over the telephone that night, seemed to echo through her quiet sitting room. Pre-suming she would be up late tomorrow night to see the old year out, she had eaten her dinner alone and had then come upstairs to read an hour or so and go to bed early.

"Whom do you wish to bring?" she asked now.

It was the girl, she supposed, and she felt a pang of ridiculous jealousy.

"My uncle, Edmond Hartley," he said. "He came home unexpectedly this morning with a queer feeling that this might be his last New Year's Eve, though he's only sixty-seven, but I don't like to leave him alone. I'm all he has, you know."

"Of course, bring him."

She spoke cheerfully enough, but she was chilled. A stranger, probably worldly wise and discerning, some-one against whom she must protect herself! She went to bed disturbed at what could only be an invasion of the privacy in which her friendship with Jared had so far been conducted. She slept fitfully through the night and

128

woke up the next morning late and ordered her breakfast sent to her room. She made no haste over the meal and it was noon before she was dressed for the day, choosing a suit she particularly liked of clear blue wool. Outside the sky was a lowering gray and the grounds, as she saw from her windows, were a darker gray, the trees, trunks and bare limbs, black with dampness. All the more reason, then, for cheer in the house, and when she went downstairs, she lit the lamps and set a match to the logs in the fireplace in the library.

About three, Jared had said, and promptly at three she saw his small car turn into the wide space between the stone pillars at the far end of the driveway. She had waited in the library, reading desultorily, and was surprised when his uncle was ushered into the library by Jared himself. She was surprised for he, Jared, had not prepared her for this handsome debonair man, tall and slim, his silver-white hair shining above a tanned face, a trim white beard, and bright blue eyes. He came forward with outstretched hands and she rose and felt her own hands clasped in a warm handshake.

"Ah, Mrs. Chardman," he exclaimed. "This is an imposition, an interruption, but my nephew insisted that I must come with him or he would stay with me, disrupting your plans, which I could not and would not allow. Besides, I was curious about you."

She recovered herself sufficiently to withdraw her hands gently. "Now I am curious about you," she said. "But I'm sure you'll want to go to your rooms first after so long a drive. Jared, Weston has put your uncle next to you. You'll share the sitting room between you."

Thus she dismissed them for the moment, with a smile and glance for Jared, and waited downstairs. Three o'clock was an awkward hour, she decided, left to herself, a space equidistant between luncheon and dinner, and the hours ahead suddenly became a burden. Three instead of two, and she could not devote herself either to Jared or his uncle! But now Jared came in alone, and stooped to lay his cheek against her hair.

"I'm leaving you to my uncle," he said. "I've an appointment with an engineer. We're to discuss something I'm making. He's a practical sort of fellow and he'll pick holes in my dreams."

"Don't let him discourage you," she said, holding his hand and looking up at him while she spoke. "I'm not sure I like people who pick holes in dreams."

"It will be good for me, and I'll be back for cocktails."

With this he put her hand to his lips and was gone, leaving her waiting and half afraid.

. . . "In fact," Edmond Hartley said, a few minutes later, "had I not been curious about you, I would not have presumed to descend upon you in this fashion." He seated himself opposite her by the blazing fire and continued. "You have had the most extraordinary effect on my nephew, Mrs. Chardman, a—a *maturing* effect, I suppose would be the best way to express it. From a most disarranged young man, not knowing what to choose among at least half-a-dozen possibilities as his lifework—and I do assure you he could be a shining success in any one of them—he is settling with a *most* interesting combination of them all, and it is something I've not really heard much about, but it appears to be extremely useful, a science and engineering sort of thing, which I confess I don't at all understand but which *seems* to me might be extremely useful. He is so much like his mother, my sister Ariadne, and again so totally *unlike* her, that I am bewildered in general, and not knowing what to do, I leave him to his own devices, and consequently, I am afraid, I have *not* been very helpful to him. But you seem to understand him so *marvelously* well, that I felt I *must* meet you, if only to thank you and, hopefully, to gain some of your wisdom."

This he poured forth in a mellifluous voice, rich in emphasis, his beautiful hands active in gesture, and his blue eyes shining, extraordinarily youthful eyes, she thought, and yet the combination conveyed a central coldness which she could not immediately fathom.

"I should like to know more about Jared's parents," she said quietly.

He looked at her. "You are so beautifully restful," he said irrelevantly. "I can see why Jared says he can always talk to you. I am not such a good listener. Indeed, as he very well knows, I usually do not know what he is talking about. My own preoccupations are early French poetry and English stained glass— cathedral glass."

"Neither of which I know anything about," she said. "And if I have done anything for Jared, it is nothing in comparison to what he has done for me. He has given me a new interest in life, which I badly needed. His youth, his enthusiasm, his energy, his extraordinary gifts are, well, quite bewildering and certainly exciting."

He leaned forward in his chair, his hands clasped on his knees. "My dear lady, may I ask? I'm his only living relative, you know. Are you by any chance— lovers?"

She hesitated before the sudden confrontation. Then she used the narrow dagger that Jared had so innocently plunged into her heart a few days ago.

"He does not think of me in that way," she said quietly.

He leaned back in his chair and his hands relaxed.

"Ah, I am almost sorry to hear you say that. He is so lonely."

She wondered, watching the mobile handsome face,

131

if she were going to dislike this man. "He told me something about a girl," she said.

"Yes, there is one in the offing—the very far offing. He's *really* not ready for marriage, I'm afraid. He's devoted to his work, as you know, and all these ideas floating about in his own mind—I doubt he is ready to undertake *any* permanent relationship. I dread it, for I saw Ariadne wither under exactly the same sort of—obliviousness, shall I say? Barnow—Jared's father—was a, well perhaps one should say he was a disorganized genius. He was highly talented, one of those brilliant men of whom in college one expects *everything,* but when they get into the practical world, all their talents disintegrate.

"Ariadne was *mad* about him. They were *both* mad, for that matter. She was a beautiful debutante. Our family was—well, it doesn't matter now, but she could have married anyone and she chose Barnow. The marriage was doomed—an exquisite girl, but spoiled—oh yes, who could *help* spoiling her? The only daughter—there were just two of us and our parents were, well, never mind, but they *were* disappointed in young Barnow as a son-in-law. I suppose divorce was just ahead, but death struck first. Barnow was on his way to an exciting new job in the West somewhere and Ariadne was with him. They were driving, and probably quarreling. At any rate, they were crossing the Rockies, one of those dreadful passes, you know, still icy in early spring, and their car went over a cliff."

"How horrible!" Her voice was a whisper.

"Horrible," he agreed, "and I thought of suing someone, for there was *no* barricade, you know. But it was explained to me that it was safer *not* to have a barricade, you know, on those heights, where *no* barricade would hold on the rocks, but people might trust to it and drive at high speed, and so if there were no barricade they would realize they *must* be careful. But being careful was one thing Ariadne never was, nor

Barnow, either. Anyway, Jared was left to me as his only relative, for my parents had died a short time before of natural causes, first my father of a cerebral something and then my mother out of sheer willfullness, I *do* believe, because she wouldn't *live* without him, and I never forgave her for it. I *adored* her and I hated my powerful, domineering father, who of course hated *me* in return and poured out his love on Ariadne. But *why* am I telling you all this about the most confusing and confused family that ever lived? Oh, yes, it's to explain Jared. So you see I've *had* to let him simply grow up in his own way, because I knew *nothing* of how to bring up a child."

"You've never married?"

"I've not been so lucky," he said abruptly.

She felt the central coldness of this man, yet not, perhaps, a basic chill so much as an absolute restraint, self-imposed in some fashion she did not as yet understand. Something was hidden in this man, he was wary in spite of his frankness.

"A tragic story," she said, "and I am glad you told me. It will help me the better to understand Jared."

She touched a bell near her and Weston came to the door.

"Put a log on the fire," she directed, "and bring us cocktails in half an hour."

She understood now why Jared was impulsive and searching everywhere for life. He had been prepared for nothing and realizing the emptiness out of which he had sprung her heart turned toward him in a fresh surge of love and compassion. She faced the ascetic figure opposite her.

"Tell me something about French poetry," she said.

. . . "I don't know," Jared said.

She was alone with him as the clock approached

midnight and the old year neared its end. An hour ago his uncle had risen to his feet.

"I *never* watch the end of an old year," he told them. "At my age it is only painful. If you will excuse me, I will thank you for a pleasant evening and take my leave."

He had bowed to her and smiled at Jared. "Good night—and sweet dreams."

"I don't know," Jared now repeated. "He wanted to come. He wanted to meet you. He said I was changed and he wanted to know why. I asked him how I was changed, and he said something was crystallizing in me, whatever that means. He lives a frightfully controlled life."

"Controlled by whom?" she asked.

"Himself. And I was wrong about his ever having a mistress. He's never loved a woman."

"He told you that?"

"Yes—when I told him about you."

"What did you tell him about me?"

"That I am hopelessly in love with you. And he said that he envied me because he'd never been in love, not with a woman, that is. And suddenly I understood him completely. He's so damnably—good. He won't accept love on any other terms but the highest. So he doesn't accept love at all. He's lived alone with his books and his paintings. Even friends he keeps at a distance. Even me."

She allowed the full tragedy of this to permeate her mind until her heart seemed physically to ache. "And do you approve of this rejection of love just because it is unorthodox?"

"Yes, I do," he said simply. "Now that I know what love is."

They looked steadfastly into each other's eyes.

"And what is love?" she asked.

"I am finding out," he said. "Someday—perhaps—I will tell you."

The minutes had slipped away as they talked and suddenly the grandfather clock in a corner struck twelve. They waited in silence, and he reached for her hands and held them in both his own. At the twelfth stroke, he stooped and kissed her lips.

"It's a new year," he said. "A new year, and in it anything can happen."

. . . But in the night she woke, and remembered everything that Jared had said about his uncle. In all her life only Edwin had been articulate about love and being a philosopher he had made even love a philosophy. Thinking of him, she could imagine him declaring in his gently dogmatic fashion that love had manifold forms, and none of these was to be summarily rejected. Thus remembering him, she found herself contrasting the two older men, Edwin so free in his own fashion within the limitless boundaries of his organized freedom and Edmond so controlled within his self-imposed restriction. Each in his own way proclaimed the supreme meaning of love, the one by acceptance and delight, the other by refusal and abstinence. The difference defined the nature of the two men, the one accepting and joyous in spite of age and infirmity, the other diffident, hiding himself in a mist of words, signifying— what? And Jared, how was it with him? Would love enlarge or confine him? For that matter, what would love do to her? Neither question could be answered as yet. She did not know the limits of love. She had only acknowledged love. She had declared, by such acknowledgment at least, its presence within her. The question now was what she would do with it—or more accurately, what it would do with her.

She lay in the silence of the night and the darkness until, oppressed, she put on the light by her bed and saw snowflakes piling on the sill of an open window and blowing softly upon the blue carpet of the floor. Getting up, she closed the window and brushed the snow into the brass fire shovel and thence upon the dead gray logs where the fire had died. She was about to get into bed, shivering with cold, when she heard footsteps pacing down the hall. She listened, wondering, and then put on her blue velvet dressing gown and opened her door. Edmond Hartley was at the head of the stairs about to descend, fully dressed, when he saw her.

"I am sleepless," he said, "and I was about to go in search of a book I saw in the library today."

"Shall I come to your help?" she asked.

"My dear lady, you are very kind."

"In a minute," she said, and returned to her mirror to brush her hair and pin it back, and touch her face with powder, her lips with color. Vanity, she told herself, but vain she was, even when she was alone. And leaving the room, she found him waiting at the head of the stair without the slightest sign of noticing that the blue of her robe matched the blue of her eyes, or that she was, in fact, quite beautiful. With an air of almost tolerant patience he allowed her to precede him down the stairs and into the library, where expertly he coaxed the dying coals in the fireplace into flames again, while she lit one lamp after another until the whole room glowed, the books on their shelves, the great bowl of flowers on the long mahogany table, the ruby red in the pattern of the Oriental rugs, the polished floor.

"Why are you sleepless?" she asked, seating herself by the fire.

He was searching a bookshelf now, his back to her.

"I am not a good sleeper at best," he replied absently, "and in a strange house—ah, here's the book I was looking for, a rare edition of Mallarmé."

"It belonged to my father," she said.

"But he was a scientist—"

She broke in, "He was everything."

"Ah, like Jared."

136

He sat down in a large armchair opposite her and opened the book. Then, not looking at her, he went on, "I've been the worst possible person to bring up a lively brilliant boy. I haven't dared to let myself love him—fearing myself, lest I love him too much—a poisonous love."

"Can love be poisonous?" she asked.

He darted a strange sidewise look at her and closed the book. "Ah, yes, indeed it can. I learned that very early. I might say I was—conditioned to it when I was very young—by an older man."

His lips seemed suddenly dry, and he ran his tongue over them. "I never thought I could ever tell that to anyone. But I want you to—to—know why I have never allowed Jared—to come close to me."

He lifted his somber eyes and in them she saw a desperate pleading to be understood.

"I understand," she said gently. "I do understand. And I think it most noble of you to—to use such restraint, such control, such reverence for true love. I respect you very much."

"Thank you," he said. "Thank you. I—I don't know if I have ever been spoken to like that before. But I have never wanted to do anything—or seem to do anything—that would warp the—the meaning of love for Jared. It was better, I thought, to let him grow up without any expression of the love I truly feel for him rather than shape a false image of love. The image of love is so easily warped—misshaped—perverted somehow, so that never again does it appear what it is, the only reason for living, the only refuge, the only source of energy and soul's growth. The very power of love— the most powerful force in life—makes love produce, when it is warped, or perverted, or even misplaced, the greatest suffering in life."

He spoke so sincerely, so deeply, that she saw him anew, a man of profound and agonized feeling, and she was silent before him.

137

"Teach him, my dear," he urged. "Teach him what love is. Only a woman can do that—a woman like you."

"I will try," she said.

. . . "I want you to come to New York and see how the hand is working," Jared said over the telephone.

She was at her desk in the library one fine spring morning, the rhododendrons outside the window already showing shades of rose and magenta as she could see. The forsythias at the far end of the lawn were in their final golden bloom, their dying brilliance gleaming against the darkness of the flanking evergreens.

"And why must I come to New York?" she asked. "You know I don't love that city."

"I know, but it's really wonderful to see how the hand is working, so well that the man is going home shortly. Besides, it will give you a reason to see my people."

She knew by now, of course, that when he said "my people," he meant the people who needed the instruments he designed to take the place of the hands and feet, the eyes, hearts, kidneys they might lose or had lost. She had scarcely seen him in the months since he and his uncle had spent the New Year with her, but his long telephone calls, made usually at midnight, and of late his short, dramatic letters, had kept him close to her. And she? It seemed that she had done nothing except play the grand piano in the music room, attend a few committee meetings and dinners and concerts, and wait until he called or wrote. She no longer hid from herself the fact that he absorbed her entire inner life and thought, so that whatever she did was of no real importance in comparison with the necessity of being there in the house when he called. Let him find her always there, ready for his every need! When he wrote, she sent her immediate, answering letter, and in this communication, at once remote and intimate, they began to use endearments that might have lit a flame had they been in each other's presence. Upon a page, in black ink, even the words "my dearest" remained cool.

"This is Tuesday," he was saying. "Can you make it tomorrow? Then we will have dinner together—maybe dance somewhere? We've never done that. Odd, I never thought of it. There's always so much to talk about when I am with you. About three? I'll meet you at the rehabilitation center—you have the address."

"Tomorrow at three," she promised.

And how absurd, she thought, five minutes later, the call ended, that she was already thinking of what she should wear! She decided on a pale gray suit with a matching coat, very thin and gracefully cut and fitting her beautifully, with hat, shoes and bag of the same silvery shade, and this gray a foil for her apple-green jade jewelry which Arnold had bought for her in Hong Kong on their last journey around the world. Thus arrayed, she left the house the next day after luncheon, the chauffeur smart in a new black uniform. Though she was accustomed to the luxuries of her life, she felt today a peculiar happiness, as though she were young again, as though she were going to meet the lover she had never had. She put from her mind every small annoyance of her life and drifted away into a mood of total happiness. For hours she would be with Jared, whom now she knew she loved as she had never loved anyone before, so that she felt herself changed and glorified by love. Do what she might, how could she hide from him the truth? But why indeed must truth be hidden?

. . . "Beautiful, isn't it?" Jared demanded proudly.

They stood in a large rectangular room, bare of decoration but bright with the afternoon sun streaming through the uncurtained windows. Around the walls were narrow hospital beds, each occupied by men with varied amputations. There was not a whole man among them, she saw as she glanced about her. Only Jared was perfect, cruelly perfect, she thought, and it was to the credit of those pallid men, lying or sitting, that there was no hatred on their drawn faces.

What Jared called "beautiful" was in fact the most hideous object she had ever seen, a two-fingered instrument on a metal arm and coated with a rubbery surface the color of human flesh.

"Let me see how it works," she countered.

"Show her," Jared commanded.

The man, very young, to whom the instrument was attached somewhere under his shirt, obeyed. The two fingers moved, separately and together, like thumb and forefinger.

"Now take her hand," Jared told him.

She controlled the instant desire to step back out of reach and instead let her hand be clasped gently by the two rubbery fingers.

"Can you *feel* her hand, how soft it is, how smooth?" Jared asked eagerly.

"Sure I can feel," the man said, and let his right eyelid drop in a mischievous wink.

She laughed and instantly every man in the room was laughing and now she did not mind at all the touch of the rubbery fingers, the forefinger stroking the palm of her hand.

"That's enough," Jared said. "You needn't carry even a good thing to an extreme."

He was laughing, too, as he spoke, but she could see he was proud.

"You have every right to be proud," she said, gently withdrawing her hand.

"Thanks—I'm happy, myself," he replied. "This fellow—he lost his right arm in Danang, didn't you, Bill?"

"Danang it was, sir. I picked up what looked like a

bunch of bananas and suddenly they went off—bang!"

Jared clapped his left shoulder.

"Well, what we've done together will help a lot of other men, too. Just remember that, will you?"

"Sure will," the man said.

They moved away then, she and Jared, away from the wounded, and in the corridor she sighed, forgetting for the moment everything except the drawn face, the skeleton-thin body of the man with the hand.

"He's so piteously young, Jared," she said.

"Not yet twenty-one," he agreed, "and I don't know a greater joy in life than to see that substitute hand working."

Absorbed in common joy, they forgot each other.

"How much does he really feel?" she asked, "and how much does his imagination supply?"

"Well, darling," Jared said with a wry smile, "I daresay he's felt many a soft hand in reality, and memory helps imagination, I'm sure—and eyesight, of course. Your hand *looks* soft, you know! But some of it's real—the pressure of a pliant material against warm flesh. Ah, yes, a good deal of it is real, enough to convey pleasure, at any rate."

What a loss, she thought, that the word of endearment he had seemed to use unconsciously had been so often carelessly used that now it was meaningless! Was it not meaningless? But he had never used it before. She stilled the sudden beat of her heart and spoke softly.

"I hope he will meet a girl someday very soon, who will be able to know what the hand you made for him can feel. Then she will think it is beautiful, too."

"I hope so," he said gravely.

He stopped at a door and took a key from his pocket and fitted it to the lock. "This is my laboratory. Remember I told you I wanted to work on the stethoscope? Well, I'm doing it."

141

He opened the door and they went in. It was a fairly large room, crowded with machinery of a delicate sort, and at one end, under the windows stood a long worktable with a chromium top. Upon it was a complex piece of machinery.

"I don't understand any of it," she told him.

"It's a method of testing stethoscopes," he explained. "Very important, you know, that a stethoscope observes accurately and reports intelligibly. It must not have what it hears distorted by some sort of vibrating sound, for example. For this I've designed a monitory microphone—this thing here—but then the listening ear must hear properly, too. I've designed this artificial ear—doesn't look much like an ear, does it? But it hears—that is, with a system like this—how much, actually, does the ear hear? How far? How clearly? But I had to check even this artificial ear with another one made of different material, and of course everything has to be checked again and again. I use recordings of the human chest wall—the heart, breathing, and so on—"

She listened, following knowledgeably enough now what he was saying, but while her brain comprehended, some other and more subtle part of her being was tensely aware of his physical nearness, his hands moving about the machinery as he demonstrated its functioning, his voice music to her ear, his profile, clear-cut against the gray walls, his whole dynamic being absorbed in what he was saying. A wave of joy swept through her being. She felt alive as she had never felt in her life before, even in her youth. They were together and bright hours lay ahead.

. . . Hours later she was in his arms. They were dancing between courses at their dinner in a famous restaurant, an after-theater place which would not be crowded until nearly midnight. They had come early, but the orchestra was already playing a slow waltz.

"I am glad," she said. "I can't do the new dances. I can't dance alone."

"And who wants to dance alone?" he retorted.

The owner-manager came up and greeted Jared by name.

"He's my uncle's friend," Jared explained.

"I like your uncle," she said.

Idle talk, but tonight she must speak only idly. They were too near the edge of something unknown, a further step toward each other, which she did not know that she wanted to take, or even whether she could stop if it began.

"Why do you tell me now that you like my uncle?" Jared demanded as they took their seats.

"I don't know, I just remember him. Perhaps I feel sorry for him."

"He's quite happy," Jared said.

He was restless, she perceived, and she did not tell him that she remembered his uncle because she pitied him, unable as he was to feel such joy as hers.

"Let's dance," Jared said restlessly.

He rose and led her to the dance floor. It had been a long time since she had danced, for Arnold had not enjoyed dancing and since his death she had not gone out. Now under Jared's superb leading she responded with all her old delight enlivened by the pleasure of new love.

"You dance beautifully," he said.

He laid his cheek gently against her hair and she yielded herself to him while she held back the words of love which waited, impatient to be spoken. Around them a few couples began to gather, but in the dim light she recognized no one and was not recognized, except that a man spoke in passing, a young blonde girl in his arms.

"Beautiful partner you have there, Jared."

"Thank you, Tim," he said coldly, and swept her

away. "I wish you wouldn't make older men envy me," he grumbled in mock annoyance.

She laughed. "But he is with a very pretty girl."

"Who wants just a pretty girl?" he retorted. "Besides, I didn't see her. I see only you."

The spell of the evening held. They sat down to a new course at the table and were silent except for a desultory few words and then he was on his feet again, inviting her, and together they returned to the communion of the dance, he pressing her to him, she yielding to his every movement. Dangerous, she told herself, dangerous but unutterably sweet. Let no word be spoken, let the communication be only this languorous delight of being close together, joined by the rhythm of music and movement. She grew afraid at last of herself, and of him. An inner wisdom restrained her. The spell must be broken now, before it was too late, now before, overcome by her own desire, she let herself be led away into some solitude when, alone with him, she could no longer control her own longing. It was near midnight and the theater crowd began to fill the room.

"I must go home," she said as a dance ended and the orchestra retired for a brief rest.

He drew himself from her reluctantly, still holding her hand in his. "Why must you?"

"What else?" she replied. "Of course I must go home."

He fell silent then, very silent. He paid the check and put her in her car, waiting at the door. He was so silent, his face was so grave as he looked at her in the dimness of the street, that she wondered if inadvertently she had hurt him. His eyes were troubled, or so she imagined, as he lingered after she was seated in the car.

"Good night," she said. "I've had a wonderfully happy evening."

"Are you sure?" he asked. "Wasn't it selfish of me to keep you entirely to myself?"

"It was where I wanted to be," she replied.

Their eyes met in a long, steadfast interchange, a communication. Sooner or later, she told herself, it must be spoken in words.

. . . She woke the next morning in a mood of resolution. The day in New York had been a double revelation. She saw Jared a man at work, she saw herself a woman in love. What had these two to do with each other, if anything? Surely something, she argued with herself. Surely love had a meaning, a purpose, but for her—what? Even before she rose from her bed, even when she had just awakened, the birds in the English ivy clinging to the walls outside the open windows of her room having roused her by their twittering and merriment, she found herself facing the questions hidden in her mind. She lay for a few minutes, her eyes closed. She must pause, she told herself, she must take thought of what she was to do with herself—and with Jared. The time of mourning for Arnold, even for Edwin, was over. Another spring had come, another love, a new life was about to begin. But what was that life to be? It was still within her power to decide, although such was her obsession with Jared that it might not be within her power if she met him again, unfortified by decision. She was dismayed to realize her own weakness. I am capable of anything, she thought in shocked dismay. I am entirely capable of seducing him. That is what I am afraid I might do! If we are alone together somewhere, some evening, even here in this house, I could do it. And he would not resist. He has passed the point of resistance. He is beginning to think of me in that way.

She was aware of a double self in this thinking. One self delighted in the possibility of seduction, oh, yes, of course a seduction so skillfully brought about that he would appear the aggressor and she the one who yielded. The other self? At this moment that one appeared as vague, as wavering as a ghost. The morning sun shone too warmly into the luxurious bedroom, the bed was too soft, her body too ready with healthy desire. She could only remember last night when, pressed to him, they had moved as one through the slow steps of the dance. For a moment she submitted to desire, then unable to endure her loneliness, she threw back the covers and got out of bed.

This daily ritual, this tending of the flesh! She stood before the mirror and twisted her long loose hair about her head and pinned it, ready for her morning shower. Then she leaned forward and examined her image. She was still beautiful in the morning, but would he ever see her so? Without makeup, she still had color, her lips softly red, a mild flush on her cheeks, her eyes blue under her lightly marked brows. She had good eyes, people always noticed her eyes, and seeing herself, she seemed to see another woman, a woman awakened to new life of some sort, the cool exterior changed, the poise gone, a tremulous, questioning, shy woman, puzzled, perhaps, or not quite daring enough. It was she, and facing herself, she was afraid again. She moved away from the image and made haste to return to the routine of bath and dress, of breakfast served as usual at the small table set for her alone in the bay window of the dining room, and Weston, waiting on her in grave silence while she drank orange juice and ate her usual meal, boiled egg and bacon and a slice of wheaten bread, without butter.

"Cook asks if you would like sweetbreads for luncheon, madame," Weston said when she rose.

"Very nice," she murmured, not caring, and she went away to her desk in the library and drew from a pigeonhole the plans for the house by the sea, a house that might someday be built, or might not. How could she know? Everything depended on the woman who would live in it, alone or not alone.

She spent the morning over the plans, finishing them to the last detail of door and window. Then, since the day continued fine, she ordered her luncheon served on the terrace and there in the shelter of the tall evergreens which hid her even from Amelia's sharp eyes next door, she sat in quiet thought while she ate, pausing now and then to toss a bit of bread to a squirrel gazing at her with sharp black eyes. When she had finished a slice of melon for dessert she rose and having made up her mind, she gave her orders.

"Weston, please have the chauffeur bring the car in half an hour. I am going to Red Hills, in Jersey."

"Yes, madame," he said.

. . . By the sea, the air was still cool. She had left chauffeur and car at the road and had walked across the dunes to the top of the cliff where the gray rock began. Here she seated herself upon a weathered log, a twisted pine which a storm had once uprooted and left. The sea was moving in mild waves, rippling into edges of white under the blue sky. The sea was blue over green depths here at the shore but deepening to purple on the horizon. Now here she was alone, and let her savor her loneliness, plumb it to its depth, its bottomless depth. For this was the evil of loving a man as she knew she now loved Jared. Love made the lover lonely without the beloved, an eternal loneliness which nothing could mend until the beloved was here again. She shrank from any other presence. How long had it been since she had sought out her old friends? Even Amelia she had not seen for weeks. She had refused all invitations, she had answered telephone calls with impatience, she had immured herself in her own obsession of love. But last night had forced her to realization. She could not continue as she was. Yet to what was she now to move for change? A question without answer!

She sighed and rose to her feet. Suddenly she wanted to descend from this height. This was too lonely a spot, poised between sky and sea. She would descend from it. She would go down the rickety steps and lie on the white sand of the beach below. Peering over the edge of the cliff, she saw a small cave under the overhanging rock. The tide was out, and the sand lay dry and warm, doubtless, from the sun. There she would hide herself, there she would escape. She glanced at the car on the road. The chauffeur was asleep behind the wheel, his cap slipping from his head and his mouth ajar. Even he would not see where she was going.

She went down the steps, clinging to the shaky rail, and stepped into the soft white sand. The cave was raised a few inches above the beach and she went to it, a place sheltered from the wind. She took off her coat and folded it into a pillow and lay down on the sand warmed by the sun. The overhanging rock made only enough shade to protect her head and shoulders, but the air was cool so that the warmth of the sun on her body was pleasant. She sighed and relaxed and felt calmed and hidden. An hour of rest would do her good. She had slept fitfully last night, had waked often. Before she was aware, she escaped now into deep sleep, soothed by the lap-lap-lapping of the waves.

. . . And was suddenly awakened by hearing her name called again and again.

"Edith—Edith—Edith!"

She opened her eyes slowly and stared up at the overhanging rock and could not imagine where she was.

"Edith—Edith!"

She sat up and shook the sand out of her hair. Her feet were wet, they were in water. And it was Jared's voice shouting at her. He was racing down the steps.

"The tide has turned, you darling idiot! I couldn't see you until you moved. Oh, how could you! How did you get here all alone? Where's your car?"

He was rolling up his trousers and preparing to wade to her.

"Take off your shoes and stockings," he commanded. "The water is only about to your knees, but a few more minutes—lucky it's a calm day! But the tide is rolling in, the cave would have filled—"

She was peeling off her stockings and now, shoes in her hand, she began to walk through the water toward him. He met her before she had reached halfway, and, his arm about her, he led her to the steps.

"Up with you as fast as possible," he scolded. "No, I'll wait until you reach the top. These steps won't bear the weight of both of us, and I don't care care to scale the cliff."

He waited, the incoming tide swelling about him, until she had reached the top and stood upon firm ground. Then he swung himself up the steps, socks and shoes in hand, and faced her. He was pale and angry.

"You might have been caught there," he shouted.

"I can swim," she said mildly and sitting on a rock she began to put on her stockings while he watched her, still angry.

"I went to your house," he said. "Weston told me where you were. Where *is* that damned chauffeur of yours?"

"He's probably wondering where I am and has gone to report me lost or something."

"You have very pretty legs and feet," he said suddenly as though he had not heard her.

"I've been told that before," she said. Then, clothed, she rearranged her hair. "I lost my hat," she continued.

"What's a hat—" he grumbled.

"Nothing, under the circumstances," she agreed, "especially as it's gone. The tide carried it away."

They were interrupted by the return of her car and with it a police car.

"She's come back," the chauffeur shouted to the

149

policeman. The two cars pulled up, and the officer stepped out and came toward them.

"I'm sorry," she told him with her best smile. "I was stupid and fell asleep on the beach. My friend, Mr. Barnow, came along and rescued me."

"Before she drowned," Jared put in.

"Before I drowned," she repeated.

The officer turned to the chauffeur. "You might have looked over the cliff!"

"I never took thought," the chauffeur said.

Jared lost patience suddenly. "While you two decide what should have been done, I will drive Mrs. Chardman home in my car. Come along, Mrs. Chardman."

She rose in a mood of strange peace and followed him and they drove away, together.

. . . "Why don't you ask me why I came?" Jared asked.

They had maintained a long silence during an early dinner at a wayside inn, a silence she had not wished to break. Indeed, she had nothing to say. The warmth of the sun, now near setting, the mild air, flowing in through the open window, the sea air, fragrant and moist, the happiness of being with him, whatever the reason, induced a profound contentment.

"Why did you come?" she asked, almost idly.

"I don't know," he replied. "I had to—I couldn't do anything else—properly, that is. You've upset me. I can't do my work—since last night. I do nothing but think about you, how you look, the sound of your voice, the way you walk. You dance better than anyone I've ever known—more gracefully. I can't tell you—it's a yielding sort of grace. I can't forget it. I've never felt like this before. Aren't you going to say anything?"

"What can I say? Except that I'm happy, wonderfully happy. I—I don't think I've ever been so happy before in my life—not in this way." Her voice drifted off in a whisper.

"In what way?" he demanded.

"If I knew, I would tell you," she said simply.

They were silent again after that. In the car the miles sped by. What he was thinking she did not know, his handsome profile stern and set, his eyes ahead on the road. But she did not know, either, what she herself was thinking. Perhaps it was not even thought, only feeling.

It was long after sunset, the darkness falling, when at last he pulled up in front of her house. Weston, hovering near the door, opened it when he heard the car.

"I didn't know what to do about dinner, madame, not hearing from you."

"We've dined," she said, "and Mr. Barnow will be staying the night—at least, I suppose so?"

She turned to Jared and he nodded.

"If you will have me—"

"Of course."

She turned to Weston. "You might bring us coffee and liqueurs in the library. I'll just go up and change."

She went upstairs exultant and afraid. Whatever was to happen would happen. She could not stay the inevitable, though she did not know what it was. She would yield, she would yield. Whatever he offered, she would take; whatever the cost, she would pay. Then upon an impulse she did not understand, she made no effort to look younger than she was. She twisted her hair carelessly upon her head, she put no makeup on her face, the sun and sea air had burned her fair skin and she let it be. She chose an old green frock and slipped it over her head and did not pause to look in the mirror. This was she, this flushed, sunburned woman with careless hair and bare feet thrust into silver sandals. She was forty-three years old and let him see her as such a woman. If he drew back, then it was her fate. But if he did not draw back? She refused the possibility. Why plan that which she could not know? She had a perverse instinct, lasting no more than a moment, when she wished that he would reject her and thus take from her the necessity for decision. She hesitated at the door, then opened it and went downstairs.

. . . He was waiting for her in the library. At the door she had hesitated again, longing and yet in dread. Then she opened it gently and only a little, but he was watching. He came swiftly across the room, he shut the door and standing with his back to it he took her in his arms and kissed her impetuously again and again.

"When I think what might have happened," he muttered.

She stood within his embrace, yielding to it, accepting, her whole body responding. Then, after a moment, she drew back. "I wasn't meant to die, it seems."

"Not if I could prevent it."

They moved hand in hand toward a sofa before which Weston had placed a small table with the liqueurs and coffee. She poured coffee, her hands shaking slightly, which he observed.

"You are trembling," he said.

"I suppose it's something of a shock," she said.

"I'm certainly shaken." He tasted neither coffee nor liqueur. Instead he began abrupt talk.

"I must tell you—I'm completely confused. I'm facing an entirely new situation. I'm committed to you. I'm not a free man any more. I've never committed myself in my life before. I've never been possessed. But now I am. I'm not even sure I like it. What does a man do when he's possessed by a woman? I only know I'd marry you tonight—if I could!"

She listened, her eyes fixed upon him. He was not thinking of her, and she realized it. He was thinking of himself, caught in a web of desire for her, resenting her because he was beginning to know how deeply he loved her. He wanted her physically and was horrified at himself. Yet if she put out her hand, if she touched him, she could have him. If she smoothed the back of his head, if she laid her hand in the curve of his arm, if she so much as looked at the slimness of waist and thigh, she could have him. She held her eyes steadfastly downcast, she refused her own desire and for reasons she did not understand except that they had nothing to do with her, but only with him, she began almost incoherently to speak out of some part of herself which, although she did not understand, she wanted him to know.

"Yesterday was such a wonderful day, Jared! I saw you as I hadn't seen you before. And I thought I knew you! We've really been together a good deal, haven't we? And yet it took yesterday, and seeing you with that amputee, to show me what you really are—a scientist, yes, and much more—a man brilliant but compassionate, strong but gentle. I love you—of course I love you—how can I help it? But it was only yesterday that made me know I love you. I shall always love you. I'm so grateful that I do. Once long ago—or it seems very long ago—a dear old man, a very great man he was, too, loved me. And he paid me a high honor. He told me that his love for me kept him alive—not only living but alive, so that his brain could stay clear and he could do his work. That, he taught me, was the great service of love—that it gives life to the lover as well as to the beloved. I've never forgotten what he taught me—about love." She was silent for a moment. Then she repeated softly what Edwin once had said. "Love keeps me not only living but alive."

He got up and walked to the tall windows and stared moodily into the shadowy gardens. A young moon rose over the pointed evergreens at the far end.

She continued, as though she talked to herself.

"I'm old enough to know that your loving me is—a

miracle. I don't understand it—I can only accept it and be grateful for it. It makes my own life beautiful. It makes me want to be useful to you in any way I can. I want to pour my life into yours, so that you'll be all you dream of being—do all you dream of doing—which you would be and do without me, of course, but perhaps my loving you, as I do, will bring you more belief in yourself than you might have had alone—I mean, without me at this moment of your life, for of course there will be many others, many people, certainly one above all—"

She broke off lest she weep. Instead she smiled at him. She lifted the small glass of benedictine and took one sip and put it down again. The words had poured forth, from what source in her being she did not know, nor did she know why she had thought of Edwin. But she was herself again, her true self, and this, too, she must wait to understand, and be content to wait.

He came back to her slowly, pausing on his way to look at a bookshelf, to examine a painting on the wall. Then he returned to her side.

"Tell me," he said. "Why was yesterday so important?"

"Because I saw the man you are meant to be," she told him. "And I will do nothing to prevent that man."

... When she was alone again, when she was upstairs in her own room, she felt dazed and yet at rest. She did not know how the words had been spoken, but they had come from a hidden part of her being. Yet now, as she recalled the moments, she realized that for a brief instant as though in a vision, she had seen side by side the man he had been only yesterday, the assured absorbed man, knowing what his work was and doing it well and finding content therein, and the man he had been today, distraught, bewildered, overwhelmed by discovering that he loved her. These two men, both of which he was, had drawn from her the words she had not known were in her, yet they were waiting to be spoken, and spoken they shaped the decision she had not known how to make. Between the two she must choose and she had chosen.

They had parted almost immediately, aware of a mutual exhaustion, and though at her bedroom door he had taken her in his arms again and kissed her, which kiss she had returned, it had been gently done, both in the giving and taking, and she knew that tonight she would open no door between them, nor would he. What she had now to do was to determine what was her place in his life. For she would love him forever. That she knew. So, knowing, what was the fulfillment of supreme love? What could it be except the fulfillment of the beloved?

She slept well that night, her inner tension released, and woke to find herself calm and rested. She lay for a while, watching the rays of the morning sun fall across the floor through the windows opening to the eastern sky. She had no sense of haste, the urgency in her was gone, and when at last she rose and made herself ready for the day, she was instinctively not surprised that Weston stood at the foot of the stairs.

"Mr. Barnow went away early this morning, madame. He left this note for you."

"I hope you gave him his breakfast," she said, with a serenity that surprised her.

"He would only have coffee, madame," Weston replied, and led the way to the breakfast room.

She followed, but not directly, pausing to go out on the terrace and breathe deeply of the fragrant morning air. The locust trees were in bloom and their fragrance had attracted the bees. Long ago, when she was a child, her father had ordered hives to be set in the far end of the garden on the theory that honey was the most healthy sweet for children and then had planted young locust trees, now grown to these giants, their rugged trunks black under the branches heavy with white blossoms. Out of tender memory she had kept the hives and each autumn the gardener removed boxes of clear white honey, still fragrant with the scent of locust.

She stood for a few minutes, looking down the aisle of trees, at the far end of which was the pool and in the pool the white marble statue of the woman standing on a rock. The scene, so familiar to her that she seldom saw it, was today as freshly beautiful as though she had been away to some far place and only now had come home again. Peace pervaded her, an inner peace which enabled her to contemplate her surroundings, yes, and even her life, with new appreciation. She had made her choice and it was a right choice and she was at peace with herself.

Alone at the breakfast table and facing the southern windows, she saw the grape arbors in full leaf, the gardener was there with a stepladder and he was trimming the vines so that the strength of the vines might produce a richer fruit. Alone, she wondered that she was not lonely. She had been so often restless without Jared. When he was not with her she listened for the telephone, she listened for the opening of a door, the sound of a voice. His habit of appearing without telling her that he was coming was exasperating but exciting and kept her tense. Yet she had never said "Let me know," for she valued his sudden need of her and his impulse to go at once to find her. When a difficulty arose in his laboratory, a technical problem or a disagreement with his superior, his recourse was to come to her and talk, until in talking he found solution, his own solution at that, for what she might say seemed to her of no importance. His lucid mind could provide its own solutions. And all this while she was holding in her hand the envelope he had left with Weston to give to her. She tore it open and drew out the single sheet it contained.

Dearest:

From now on that is what you are to me. No matter who else comes—or goes—that one word is what you are, and will always be, to me. No change is possible. Why you said what you said yesterday, why you did what you did, I do not ask, because, whatever the reason, it was right. I know.

I am yours always,
Jared

She folded the sheet and put it back in the envelope. When she went to her sitting room she would lock it in her desk to keep and to read again and again. Their love was established in the only way it could be established. She need never again wait or listen for his coming. She understood why he had left her today and she knew that he would always come back. She had made it possible for him to return to his work. She had given him his freedom even from love, and so he would love her forever. Thus musing, and smiling to herself, she ate her breakfast and thought of him with peace. Only of him she thought as she went about her day. With no planning for the future she thought of him and felt alive and strong and well.

. . . At the beginning of May, when the pink and white dogwoods were in bloom, the season that year being somewhat late, she had a telephone call from a girl. She knew at once it was a girl for the voice that came singing over the wire was the freshest, most youthful voice she had ever heard and she knew she had not heard it before.

"Mrs. Chardman?" the voice inquired.

"It is I," she replied.

"Yes, well, I don't know how to begin, but I am June Blaine. You don't know me but I know Jared Barnow. I'm his friend—sort of!"

"Yes?"

"Yes! And I want most awfully to talk with you."

"About him?"

"Yes, about him."

"Does he know?"

"I told him I was calling you today."

"And?"

"He said you would understand his point of view so it would be all right. He says you're the only person who really knows him. That's what he thinks! But I know him, too."

She was silent for a few seconds when the voice stopped speaking. Then she said quietly, "Very well. When?"

"This afternoon?" the pretty voice inquired.

"At four o'clock," she said.

"Oh, thanks!"

The telephone clicked, the voice was gone. She considered a moment and then dialed the laboratory. At eleven o'clock in the morning Jared would be there. His voice answered almost immediately.

"Jared Barnow."

"It is I," she said. "A girl just called. She wants to see me. This afternoon."

"That's June," he said quickly. "We were playing tennis last week at her place and she wanted to know if she could see you. I said why not. Don't take her seriously, darling. She wants to marry me and she hasn't a chance. I'm too preoccupied!"

She laughed. "Go back to your work, then! By the way, I've been reading a fascinating article on silicone rubber implants for replacing arthritic or destroyed joints in human hands."

"I saw that. Heat—molded implants—wonderful."

"Yes, well, I won't keep you."

"I'll call you tonight."

He called her every night now at midnight when he ended his day. If he waked her, as sometimes he did, she never let him know. If he called her, it meant he needed her.

"Do call me," she said now, and put up the receiver.

. . . She was not restless while she waited for four o'clock, but she was stone silent. She did not try to busy herself. Instead she lay in a long chair on the terrace, submitting herself, her eyes closed, her body motionless. Clouds drifted over the blue sky, great billows of white, and she felt the chill of shadows as they passed, and then between them was the warmth of the sun. A cool mild wind rippled over the trees and passed, leaving a motionless quiet behind. Sometimes she was almost asleep but never quite. When Weston asked where she would have her luncheon, she said, "Bring it to me here, please." And when he had brought it she left it half eaten.

Once or twice, perhaps more, she got to her feet and walked about the lawns. The thick growth of late spring shielded her from everyone, even from Amelia, whom she had not seen in weeks. But she always returned to the long chair and lay down, waiting, while the sun rose to its zenith and passing, moved westward.

And then promptly at four o'clock she heard the sound of a car driven to the entrance on the other side of the house, and the doorbell rang and she knew she had been waiting all day for this moment. She did not move, but continued to lie waiting, her eyes still closed, for the sound of footsteps, Weston's soft shuffling and the clip clip of a girl's heels.

"Miss Blaine has arrived, madame," Weston said.

She opened her eyes. There the girl stood, a tall slim creature in a very short white dress, a girl with green eyes and tawny hair hanging shining and straight to her shoulders, a girl with a clean, well-bred look but one with a stubborn mouth, unsmiling. She pulled off her short white gloves and put out her right hand and spoke in a decided but pleasant, rather light voice.

"Please don't get up, Mrs. Chardman."

"I wasn't going to, June, is it? I'm lazy today."

"Yes, it's June. For the obvious reason that I was born in June. I'll be twenty-one next month."

"Draw up a chair and sit down, June."

"Thank you."

She drew up a chair and sat down, her back to the garden and facing the graceful woman in the long chair.

"You're younger than I thought, Mrs. Chardman."

"Oh, no—I'm as old as you think I am. Didn't Jared ever tell you how old I am?"

"No. He always talks of you as if you were his age."

"That's kind of him."

A pause, and the girl's eyes were on her face, she could feel the steady gaze as she continued to look down the long vista of the gardens. Then she made an effort and met the watching eyes.

"Tell me about yourself, June—why you want to see me, anything you like, tell me."

The girl's voice was casual, deliberate, clear. "I'll come straight to the point. I want to see the sort of woman Jared likes. I want to know if you are anything like me. Or must I—sort of—recondition him to another woman—like me."

She laughed. "Is that what you think you can do, June?"

"I'll try, if I must!"

"In other words, you're determined to—marry him?"

"If I can."

"Do you think you can?"

"Yes."

The girl's voice was quite calm, quite firm.

160

"Then there's nothing more to be said, is there, June?"

"Yes, because I want him to love me first."

"And do you think he can be taught to love you?"

"I will teach him, as soon as I know how. That's why I've come to you. You've done it. He loves you. But of course he can't marry you. You're too old. Still, he'll have to marry someone. I want to be that someone. That's why I'm here."

She was amazed, amused, wounded and even somewhat angry. An instinct of self-defense and perversity compelled her, almost, to defy the girl, to say carelessly with a laugh if she could muster laughter, that she might just marry Jared herself. It had been thought of!

"Did Jared say I am too old to marry him?"

"He's never mentioned marriage to me. I don't believe he's thought of marrying anyone. I'll be the first one."

This was said with such self-confidence that again she wanted to laugh and could not. And of course the girl was right. She was too old to marry Jared. Women nowadays did often marry men much younger than themselves, but there was something repulsive in the idea. Love—but not marriage! One couldn't help loving a certain human being, and it might have nothing to do with marriage. Edwin had taught her that.

"Please teach me," the girl said.

"Do you love Jared?" she asked.

"Of course," the girl said. "Else why would I bother myself about him?"

"What is it you love about him?"

"Everything," the girl said.

"Define everything, please!"

"Well—just everything. The way he walks, the way he talks, the way he looks—it's just a sort of magic."

"It's not everything. It's only the outside of him."

"Well, that's enough for me."

"Ah, but is it enough for him?"

The girl looked at her stubbornly, her green eyes unwavering. "It's enough to begin on."

She returned the girl's gaze. "Perhaps it is," she said. And then after a moment she said, "How can I know why Jared loves me? Why don't you ask him? Certainly it's not because of the way I walk—or talk—or even because of some sort of magic—which I don't have, I'm sure. I can't help you, June. I don't know how."

She wanted suddenly to be rid of this girl. She was angry with her—the absurdity of such a visit, the insolence of the intrusion! Young people nowadays thought only of themselves. Yes, she was too old, too old for Jared, too old for this girl.

She rose and walked toward the door. "I'm afraid I can't help you, my dear. I really don't know what you're talking about. You and Jared must settle your own relationship. Now come in and have a cup of tea with me. Or would you rather have something to drink?"

. . . It was dusk when the girl left. Hours had passed and she had let them pass, had helped them to pass, because she had reluctantly begun to like this girl. There had been nothing new in her story, for she told it without being asked. Divorced parents, she an only child, about to graduate from a girls' college.

"I try to be fair to both my parents, Mrs. Chardman, but I live in my father's house because my mother has married again and I don't like my stepfather. He's younger than my mother and sometimes—well, I don't like to be where he is, because I don't want my mother to be hurt—not by me, and certainly not by him because she's terribly in love with him. It's so pitiful, isn't it?"

"Where did you meet Jared?" she had asked the girl.

"When we were skiing three years ago. I love to ski.

162

Usually I spend Christmas holidays skiing. Now we play tennis. It was so surprising to find he lives in New York and I live in Scarsdale, you know. He comes to our place on Saturdays sometimes, unless he calls up that he wants to work. My father and he are good friends. My father says he's the most brilliant young man he's ever known."

"What does your father do?"

"He's a banker in New York. He has an apartment there and I can stay with him if I like, but we've kept our house in Scarsdale because we like tennis and the pool and all that."

"He hasn't married again?"

"Oh, yes—a girl not much older than I—well, Louise is twenty-six."

"They're happy?"

"Oh, yes, Louise is so beautiful that I'm glad she didn't see Jared before she married my father. But all these marriages have taught me such a lot, Mrs. Chardman. I don't want ever to be divorced. I want to marry someone I shall always love—like Jared."

"You must also be someone he can always love," she said.

"Oh, yes," the girl agreed. "That's why I've come to you. He says he'll love you forever."

. . . "Your little girl spent the afternoon with me," she told Jared that night at midnight.

"I have no little girl," he retorted.

"Well, *a* little girl, then!" she laughed.

"I suppose you mean June Blaine."

"Yes!"

"Yes, well, she's the one I once told you about. It's been off and on for a couple of years and now it's off."

"She doesn't think so."

"She's strong—that I admit. But all girls are strong these days."

163

"And you don't like that?"

"Haven't time to think about it. What are you doing this weekend?"

She hesitated, searching for an excuse, even a mild lie. "I've promised an old friend."

"Man?"

"No—woman." She could summon Amelia and they could go to the summer theater.

"Well—" He was reluctantly giving up the weekend.

"Perhaps June—" she suggested.

He broke in sharply. "Look here—don't you go matchmaking!"

"Of course not, it's just loyalty to one's kind."

"I'm your kind!"

"I know that, darling, but—"

"No buts!"

"Very well. Shall we say good night on this moment of agreement?"

"I don't know. You seem different, as though the agreement were only skin deep."

"Ah, no, Jared! It's very deep. I'm *for* you—ever and ever. There's no agreement deeper than that."

She could hear him draw a deep breath.

"That's what I wanted to hear. Now I can say good night."

"Good night, dearest."

Like an echo his voice came back to her—

"Dearest!"

. . . "I hear Edmond Hartley was at your house," Amelia said.

They were sitting midway to the tent-like ceiling of the theater-in-the-round in a suburb of the city. Amelia had decided on the play, a revival of an old musical.

"How did you know?" she asked.

"Oh, our built-in intercom," Amelia replied. "Your

164

chauffeur to mine and then to my upstairs maid who brings my breakfast when I'm too lazy to get up."

"Does Edmond Hartley interest you?"

"Once he did—very long ago—until I found out I didn't interest him. No woman does. But he was charming in spite of that—and rich!"

"He's still charming."

"And not married?"

"No."

This was in the intermission. Amelia had declared that it was absurd to climb down the steps and up again in such a crowd. Besides, there was nowhere to go. She began once more.

"Do you know, Edith, I sometimes wonder if marriage with a man like that, at our age, anyway, wouldn't be rather pleasant. One would have companionship, someone to travel with, a friend always present—and no demands!"

"I couldn't endure it," she said vehemently.

"Why not?"

"I'd want all of marriage—or none."

Amelia made shrill laughter. "You're confessing, Edith, you're confessing!"

"I have nothing to confess except a deep respect for love."

"Well, I'd settle for diversion," Amelia said.

The audience was swarming up the aisles again and there was a bustle on the stage. But the conversation was background for the following week, the last of June. A letter written on heavy cream paper with embossed name and address announced that the sender was Edmond Hartley, asking if he might call upon her, "to pay my respects," the next Tuesday, on his way to Washington to judge designs for murals to be placed in a museum there. She would have replied that she was engaged, except that she thought of Amelia.

"And an old friend of mine," she added as postscript

165

to her own answering letter, "will be here to greet you. I believe she knew you long ago. Do come!"

He came late on Tuesday afternoon, in a small Daimler limousine, driven by an elderly English chauffeur. She saw him arrive and pause to direct the man and then he walked in his sprightly somewhat mincing fashion to the door. Weston opened it and announced him in the music room. She rose from the piano, where she had been working on a Chopin *étude,* and put out her hands, which he took in his cool dry grasp.

"How beautiful the music sounds! This is my favorite *étude.* I must hear it all."

His eyes were as brightly blue as ever above his white clipped beard and trim mustache. A handsome man, she thought, in his precise, delicate fashion, and she felt a mild affection for him, combined with a real respect. A complicated personality, this! But under the complexities, the result of untold experience, here was an honorable person who had dealt rigorously with himself.

"My dear," he said, "I am dusty with travel. Let me make myself fit for your beautiful eyes."

"Then we'll have cocktails on the east terrace," she said. "And my old friend, Amelia Darwent, will join us. Do you remember her? She remembers you very well indeed."

Edmond Hartley looked blank. "I don't remember—"

"Ah, well, she will recall herself to you. Now go upstairs—the same room and sitting room."

He went away and she returned to the *étude,* the third. She had begun it after Arnold's death, when she was learning the meaning of sorrow, and not only the sorrow of death but the deeper sorrow of knowing that what had been was not all that it could have been had there been more understanding and therefore more communication between Arnold and herself. They had both done the best they could together. If she realized there might have been a deeper happiness, so had he. Of that she was sure, for she had sometimes felt his gaze upon her and, lifting her head, had seen sadness in his eyes, and silently had respected that sadness, comprehending in her own reserve the inexorable distance between them. Neither she nor Arnold had overcome that reserve, but the knowledge and acceptance were painful.

Upon the day of his funeral, she had returned to this house alone, for she longed to be alone and rejected the affectionate offers of her children to come home with her. "No, my dears," she had told them. "Go home to your children. Be with them, and I shall be happy. Indeed, I am quite all right. I'll take a sleeping pill tonight—I am very tired"—and there alone she had begun the *étude*. It was divided into three parts, the first the statement of sorrow, a query as to why the sorrow must be. In the second part question rose to protest and wild demand. In the closing third, the question was unanswered, the demand unheeded and the theme was expressed again and finally, this time by acceptance of the inexorable.

When the last chord died under her hands, she heard Amelia's voice.

"If I had a heart, it would break when you play that."

She turned. Amelia was sitting in a gold chair, looking very smart in a cocktail dress of silver lamé.

"When did you come?" she asked.

"Ten minutes ago. I wouldn't let Weston announce me. I haven't heard you play for a long time—months. You play better than ever, Edith. I'm furious with my parents that they didn't make me keep practicing."

"As I remember it," she said, smiling, "you hated them for making you practice for two years."

"They shouldn't have listened to my complaining," Amelia insisted. "They should have beaten me. As it is, I blame them for my not having the ability now to

167

comfort myself with music. They should have had more backbone."

"They wanted their only daughter to love them."

"A stupid way to win love! They should have known that the only way to be loved is to be stronger than the one you love."

"I never before heard you talk about love, Amelia."

"That's not to say I have no ideas on the subject!"

They were interrupted by the arrival of Edmond Hartley. He had changed his suit to a tan surah silk, and he wore jade cuff links and tie pin. Amelia put out her hand.

"Well, Edmond!" she said, surveying him. "You're handsomer than ever."

He returned her gaze and she released his hand.

"Now I remember you," he said. "You're the girl who always beat me at tennis!"

He turned. "This young woman, Mrs. Chardman, had the most evil backhand. And she was quicksilver on her feet. I was agile, or so I thought, but she was fleet as—as a—young gazelle, and I simply could not win. I could never make up my mind whether to love her or hate her!"

Amelia laughed in delight. "You never did make up your mind," she declared.

"I never did," he agreed.

They looked at each other, comparing themselves as to age. How had the years dealt with them, and with which the more kindly? An old attraction stirred. As nearly as he had ever come to marriage he had once nearly married Amelia Darwent. Each of them now remembered.

. . . That night when Jared called she told him, half in amusement, "Your uncle, Jared, is reviving an old attraction. Love is too strong a word. But he and Amelia once knew each other. They forgot and now remember again. He went away after dinner, but I heard him ask Amelia if he might call upon her tomorrow."

Jared shouted laughter. "It's as far as he will go, bless him!"

To her own surprise, she was suddenly annoyed with him. "Don't laugh, Jared! He's a tragic man—and a good man."

"Of course he's good, but—"

"No but! He's come to terms with himself, and knowing himself, he's refused the best life can give."

"That being—"

"Love, of course. How young you are," she said almost contemptuously and her heart began suddenly to ache.

"I don't understand you," he said, very blunt.

"There's no need to," she replied.

. . . Deliberately during the next few days she devoted herself to Edmond Hartley and Amelia. Seeming to see nothing, she saw everything. She understood Amelia so well and so affectionately. Amelia had always been direct and never was she more direct than now. She walked across the lawns and appeared at odd hours, always beautifully dressed for the time of day, looking handsome in her somewhat severe fashion, her stubborn gray hair fashionably cut, her skirts short enough to reveal her shapely legs. Black and white suited her, and she wore white for the warm summer days and long diaphanous black gowns in the evening. Her abrupt ways, her clipped speech, combined with her almost ostentatious deference to Edmond, obviously touched and pleased him. It had been a long time since a woman had paid him attention. He ceased to shrink from being alone with her and began to suggest a stroll through the trees. Amelia accepted each invitation immediately and it became almost usual that before the cocktail hour Edith saw the two tall figures, Edmond an inch or two the taller, strolling arm in arm about the grounds. She was prepared, therefore, for Amelia's forthright announcement one evening in July.

"Edith, I've just asked Edmond Hartley to marry me."

"Amelia, have you really?" she exclaimed. "And what did he say?"

Amelia gave her short bark of laughter. "He couldn't very well refuse, could he, without being impolite, so he said he considered it an honor and accepted."

They were in her upstairs room, whither Amelia had followed her. She was lying on the chaise longue, resting for half an hour before dressing for dinner.

"Amelia, I suppose you know—"

Amelia finished the sentence impatiently. "That he's not interested in sex with a woman? Yes, I know—I've always known. Why do you suppose I've never married? I was mad about him when we were young. He was the handsomest man in the world. Then he told me, yes, Edith, he *told* me! I've always admired him for that. He's so—decent. He understood himself, he had himself in hand. He was never going to let himself—well, you know! He was simply going to live without sex. It was so brave of him. Wasn't it brave? Yes, and so I have, too. You'll think it silly and old-fashioned of me. But there simply hasn't been another love for me, either, and sex without love just doesn't—well, appeal to me. Of course for a while I was shocked, even repelled, healthy beast that I was. We didn't see each other for a long time. But gradually during the years I've come to see that sex isn't all that matters between people and gradually sex has been drained away. What's left now is love. That's what I said to him. 'Edmond, I love you. You, yourself. I want to live in the same house with you, be near you, that's all.' He said, as I told you, that 'it would be an honor.' "

She thought she had known Amelia from earliest

memory and now perceived that she had not known her. So many years she had been wrong, but now she understood her friend and with understanding she felt a real love for a sister woman.

"I respect you both," she said quietly. "When will you be married?"

"As soon as we can arrange the legalities," Amelia told her. "Then Edmond will move into my house. We've discussed everything. He can have the east wing for himself. There will be plenty of room to hang all his paintings. Edith, I can't tell you how happy I am. I'm glad I had the courage to face the truth we've always known, that we ought to spend our lives together. He's so—honorable. He would never have asked me. So I put aside false modesty and all that, and I asked him."

"Then I am glad, too," she said.

Amelia had opened a door and revealed a secret chamber.

. . . "I want you to marry," she told Jared. She had pondered constantly upon Amelia's courage and from it had drawn strength.

Unconsciously he drove more quickly. It was a Sunday afternoon in midsummer and he had appeared suddenly unannounced to take her to a country inn to dinner. She had been alone and a trifle at loose ends, for Amelia three days ago had announced that she and Edmond were going to Europe, after a brief and inconspicuous wedding ceremony. No, she would not tell even her dear friend Edith Chardman where they were going, nor exactly when, but they would be in touch with her upon their return. The next day Amelia's big house was closed, except for a caretaker. She missed Amelia more than she had thought possible, for the last link with her childhood was gone and no other took her place. Even the thought of her son and daughter did not relieve her loneliness. They had their own lives and she had hers apart by generation and sophistication. Their stage was the procreation of children and the establishment of their own family structures, whereas she—at what stage was she? Time and space surrounded her as a solitary traveler upon a desert is surrounded by sand and sky. She felt so weakened indeed by inner loneliness that she had almost wept when Jared telephoned her to propose this evening journey.

"I want you to marry," she repeated when he did not reply.

Instead of speaking, he pulled up abruptly in the overhanging shade of a huge ash tree. It was that moment in summer when growth is ended, and nature contemplates the annual death of winter. The air was languid and birds were silent.

"Now," he said, "let's have this out. I shall never love anyone as I love you."

"I accept that," she said, "and still I say I want you to marry."

"Will you marry me, Edith?"

"No," she said gently.

"Why not?"

Easy enough to say simply that she was too old, that when he was in his prime she would be an aged woman, but she did not reply simply. There was between them the communication of a love that had nothing to do with the accident of birth. They were two human beings who recognized their complete congeniality, their total trust, which were the components of love. Nevertheless, she had a responsibility of which she was becoming aware, at first dimly but now, day by day, more clearly. Nothing must impede the fulfillment of Jared's whole development as a man, rich in talents and capable of rich growth, mental and spiritual. Yet he was a man, a human creature, with human needs. These needs she could not totally fulfill, and were they not so fulfilled, could the final development take place?

She believed not. She could not live with him as an everyday wife. She could not give him children. Indeed she had no wish so to do. And yet, had she been able, could she also have given what she now gave him so joyously in companionship? She doubted that she could. He was no simple creature. The spectrum of his being was radiantly total and she comprehended the totality.

"I know I cannot marry you, Jared," she said now.

"Are you afraid of what people will say?"

"I am not afraid," she told him.

"Then why?"

"I know I must not."

"Why, why?"

"I don't know, but I must not, for your own sake."

He was silent after this, and she was silent, waiting. Then he put the car into gear and drove on, until they reached the country inn, once an old mill. The great dark waterwheel still turned slowly, dripping the clear brook water as it had done for a century and more. The wood was covered with wet green moss, and under the shade of a huge overhanging sycamore tree, the water slipped smoothly over the stones and on its way to the river.

They stood side by side for moments, she and Jared, watching the turning wheel. Suddenly he seized her hand resolutely and drew it into the crook of his arm.

"Come along," he said. "I'm starved."

They entered the dining room together and in his imperious fashion he declined the table to which the waitress led them.

"That table by the window," he ordered.

They sat down, he decided upon cocktails and entrée, while she waited in acquiescence, not caring what she ate and drank so long as she was with him. Of course she loved him. Yes, she was in love with him.

173

No, she would never separate herself from him. One after the other these facts announced themselves in her being, but did not in the least or in total change her decision.

He leaned on his elbows and faced her, his eyes bleakly dark. "Now, then," he said, "let's have it out. Why do you insist upon my marrying someone?"

"Not someone," she amended. "Just June Blaine. I like her. She's honest. She wants to marry you."

"I know that, but—"

"No buts! Of course the final decision is yours, but I want you to know that I—approve."

He stared at her, puzzled. "I don't understand you."

She smiled and was silent.

He continued. "You know—you and I—"

She broke in. "I know."

His eyes, so direct in their gaze, held her prisoner. She could not look away.

"Will I ever understand you?" he demanded.

"Perhaps it's not—necessary." Her voice faltered.

"Nevertheless, I'd like to," he persisted.

"Not—necessary," she repeated, her voice a whisper.

"Now you're hiding somewhere," he declared.

She shook her head. "Just being—myself."

"I don't like mysteries!"

"No mystery, Jared, perhaps intuition. I know you so well—better than I know myself, I think! I see so clearly what you are and what you will be. You will be one of the few great men of your generation—even of all generations, I think! Nothing must go wrong. You must have—everything. And June will be part of that everything. And I tell you, I *like* her! One doesn't find honesty in women too often these days. It's like finding a diamond among pebbles. You can't pass it by. You must not. You must take it in your hand, examine it, test it, and if it's true, keep it. That's all I'm asking—no, I don't ask, I suggest."

"I won't even talk about it," he said bluntly. "Here are our cocktails. I drink to *you!*"

And he lifted his glass.

. . . Hours later, lying awake in her bed, she turned to the telephone on the table beside her and lifting the receiver, she dialed June, guessing that she, too, was sleepless, and heard her voice, instant and alert.

"Yes?"

"June, it is I, Edith Chardman."

"Yes, Mrs. Chardman?"

"I want to tell you I am going away for a few weeks—maybe months."

"Is there something you want me to do?" June's voice spoke puzzlement.

"Only what your heart tells you, while I am gone."

She waited. Was June perceptive enough, quick enough, understanding enough, to know what she was saying?

A moment of silence and the girl's answer came, quiet and controlled.

"Thank you, Mrs. Chardman."

"Good night, my dear," she said and put the receiver back in its place.

. . . In the morning she rose late, rested after deep sleep. She had been able to sleep at once after the telephone call to June, as though she had fulfilled a duty, a purpose, and having fulfilled, had relaxed into peace. Now, the sun already nearing zenith, she got up and went to the window, as she always did in the morning, to judge the day, in this case a perfectly clear August day, the cloudless sky blue above the trees. It was a day to strengthen her soul with its beauty and she was strengthened. She had told June she was going away, but where would she go? Until the moment she had spoken the words she had had no intention of going away. Yet those very words had risen to her lips with conviction, as though they were the fruit of meditation and resolution. Where could she go? Standing irresolute before the open window, the morning breeze stirring the filmy folds of her long nightgown, and lifting her loosened hair, she suddenly thought of Edwin's house in the mountains, two hundred miles away.

Perhaps it stood empty, perhaps his children were there, perhaps anything, but at least she would go and see. No one could find her there, and she had never told Jared of that love, nor indeed anyone. Then she would go and in the presence of Edwin's memory, she would find herself again, not as she had been, for love had changed her, love for Jared, but as she was now to be until the end of her life. For there would never be another love. She had known them all, each love different from the other, each meaningful, each illuminating and valuable and to be cherished. Nor was it ended. Her love for Jared would continue for she had no wish to stop it. Let it grow, a source of comfort and inspiration to her, as hers had been for Edwin, but with even greater responsibility. She must assume that responsibility—it was now to make love a source of comfort and inspiration to Jared. The torch of love must be handed on from one heart to another, from one generation to the next, for without love life was meaningless and the spirit died. Yes, that was her duty and her delight, to pour her love into Jared's life and see him grow. It was not a love affair. It was love.

. . . The great house stood silent in the golden light of late afternoon. The heavy door was locked. There, where Edwin had always stood to welcome her, his arms outstretched to enfold her, no one stood. The flower beds were neglected, early chrysanthemums and late roses blooming in bright confusion. A bird called, its lonely cry piercing the stillness. She lifted the huge

176

brass knocker and let it fall and heard the echo inside the hall. She waited. Surely someone must be here, a watchman, a caretaker, a housekeeper? The house stood alone, five miles from the nearest village, a solitary road leading to the gate. With its treasures of books and paintings, the furniture of a lifetime rich in possessions, it could not stand untended here on this hill, surrounded by forests and beyond the forests, mountains. Five peaks were clear against the evening sky, two of them already tipped with early frost.

Now from a distance within the house she heard footsteps, now the grating scrape of a metal bar, or perhaps of a large key—she could not remember. The door opened a few inches, and she saw the gnarly face of Henry Haynes, Edwin's manservant.

"Why, Mrs. Chardman!" His grainy voice had not changed. "Whatever—"

"Can you put me up for a week—or two—or three?"

"Well, now—"

He opened the door wide. "Come in. There's nobody here but my wife and me. I married the cook. I don't know as you remember her. Dr. Steadley put her in his will and it seemed easy just to—come in, Mrs. Chardman. The family was here for the summer but they've all gone and we was settling ourselves in for the winter."

He led the way as he talked. She stood in the wide hall and looked about her. Everything was the same, the furniture polished, the floors dustless! There was even a bowl of golden chrysanthemums on the hall table, a great Satsuma bowl, which she remembered well, for Edwin had found it in Japan. Yet how empty the house was!

She stood hesitating. Could she bear his absence here in this house? The loneliness was too intense. She felt solitary as she had never felt before, not even when Arnold died and left her alone in her own house.

Edwin had meant more to her than she had realized. Would the loneliness of his absence now overwhelm her, make her afraid?

"Everything is like when he was here," Henry was saying. "Beds made, fires laid—everything. I even took out his winter things yesterday and aired them. My wife says, 'Henry, he don't know,' but I know, I tell her, I know. Shall you have the same room, Mrs. Chardman?"

"Yes, the same."

She followed him up the stairs and down the hall to the remembered door. He opened it and she went in.

"It looks exactly as it did," she said.

"And will always be," Henry said. "He wants it like that. 'Henry,' he says, 'keep it like it always was. I don't know if I can come back, but keep it as if I could!' So I keep it, books dusted, everything."

"Perhaps he knows," she murmured.

Now that she was here, she was tired, she realized. She took off her hat and saw her face in a mirror, white and tired.

"You'll have dinner early as possible," Henry said. "I'll tell my wife. It'll be good to have something to do."

"Thank you, Henry," she said.

When he was gone, she unpacked her two bags and put things away into drawers.

But I needn't stay, she thought, I can just go away at any moment, any day, if I can't bear it. Only where would I go?

She sat down before the small mahogany desk near the western window. The sun was setting, it seemed at this moment to rest upon the rocky peak of the highest mountain, and she watched it sink until the last edge of gold was gone. Then she lit all the lamps in the room and put a match to the logs in the fireplace, and having done so, felt herself somehow at home, though still alone.

. . . The first early snow was falling, although the last bright leaves were still clinging to the maple trees when she put aside the curtains of her bedroom one morning and saw the large soft flakes drifting past the window. Henry had turned up the furnace.

She drew back the curtain and fastened it, and a white light filled the room. She lit the fire, the logs piled ready in the chimney piece, and slowly, luxuriously, she showered and dressed and went downstairs to breakfast. There in the breakfast room Henry had lit a fire and had moved a small table beside it.

"It's sharp this morning," he said.

"It's beautiful," she said.

"Dr. Steadley always liked snow."

"I know."

"It's queer how he still seems to be in this house," Henry said.

"Do you feel it, too?" she asked.

"Times I come in, I almost hear his voice," Henry said.

"If you believe he is here, then to that degree he is here," she replied.

She was aware of a strange confidence as she spoke. If any presence could be believed, surely Edwin was that one. But she was a skeptic. What had been was no more. He had left this shell, this habitation, behind him and was gone. She was singularly alone, more alone, she reflected, than if she had never lived here with him. Nor did she wish him back. She had come here to learn how to live alone, and she pressed her loneliness into her heart and flesh. She was alone, alone, so wrapped in her solitary being that she did not even notice that Henry had left the room.

. . . The solitary days passed, one after the other in a gray procession. Since no one knew where she was, there were no telephone calls. She spent her waking hours in the huge library, studying books she had never read before, books of Asian history and philosophy. Edwin had traveled much in that part of the world, and now she began to understand how much Asia had shaped his character. The natural freedom, the ease with which he had accommodated the physical with the philosophical, was Asian. The body was only the manifestation of the spirit, translating into terms of flesh and blood, pulse and heartbeat, the yearnings of the spirit. The need for physical love was only a materialization of the spirit's craving for communication. There was no essential difference between flesh and spirit, simply a difference in mode of expression.

Jared had not progressed so far, however. Nor indeed had she. Flesh was of the flesh. When she thought of Jared in the flesh, she thought of his body. His spirit was apart. She could and did think of his spirit, but it was something in itself. Spiritually he was a creator. Just now, of course, he was only a beginner. He was creating tools, mechanisms to satisfy his creative compulsion. He had to make something with his hands, something he could see and use, a noble instinct, but on a first level. His creativity was motivated by compassion, a worthy instinct, but not strong enough in itself to reach the fulfillment of his capacity as a creator. In days gone by, the creator always found his fulfillment in art, but now the greatest artists were scientists. Science was so exciting, so new, so all but insuperable that it challenged every creative mind. She had no doubt that if he were not impeded, Jared would grow into a great scientist.

If he were not impeded! But no one could impede him except her, herself. Somehow she had come into his life at a moment when he needed to worship and he had worshiped her. What does a woman do with a man's worship? She can destroy it by her own selfish need—or she can use it for his development and growth.

I must never let him know, she thought.

But know what?

She must never let him know that she was merely woman. She must never descend to daily need, if she wanted to keep him. No, even that was selfish. There could be no question of "keeping." She must rise to heights of her own. She must be quite willing to release him while she loved him—even because she loved him, for love, if it be true, seeks only the fulfillment of the beloved and this on the highest level.

Slowly, day after day, she moved her way dimly to a new definition of love, eliminating every trace of selfishness in order that she might find the purest satisfaction. Slowly she rejected even loneliness and became no more alone but absorbed in her search for the substance of love in its essence. And all during this search she did not write to Jared or telephone him. She needed to be alone in order to outlive loneliness. When she was no longer lonely, she would find him again, or he would find her.

In such mood the days passed in the silent house. Days passed in which she spoke to no one except to acknowledge Henry's greeting, or answer his wife's occasional question.

"Is everything all right, Mrs. Chardman?"

"Yes, thank you, Margaret."

"Is there anything you would fancy to eat?"

"No, thank you. Whatever you prepare—it's quite all right."

Days passed into weeks. The snow fell heavily now and settled into permanence. Winter loomed. She wondered if she should return to her own house, and did not. Edwin was gone, and she lived entirely in the presence of Jared. He was no longer the young man from whom she had withdrawn herself. Slowly she came to see him as the man he would be someday, Jared the fulfilled, Jared the creator, master of himself, imaginative, dedicated, uncompromising in his creativity. He had become one of the few great men of his time, his acts of creation of art were no longer mere inventions. How would she know his greatness? When artist and scientist combined in him, he would be that great man.

. . . "Now I have found you," Jared said.

He announced himself by arrival. She was at the piano that morning when the doorbell rang. She stopped to listen, she waited for Henry or Margaret to open the door but neither appeared. Then she opened the door herself and Jared stood there in the rain. Three days of rain had washed away the last snowfall.

"Have you been looking for me?" she asked.

"Everywhere. No one could tell me where you were."

"Because I told no one."

"You wanted to hide from me!"

"Come in out of the rain."

She threw the door wide, he shook himself, and came in, and took off his raincoat and hat. At the same moment Henry appeared, astonished at a guest, and taking both hat and coat, looked at her with inquiring eyes.

"Yes, Henry," she said. "Mr. Barnow will be here— for the night, Jared?"

"If you'll have me, but tomorrow I am taking you home."

She did not reply to this, but led the way to the living room. The wind from the open door had blown the sheets of her music about, and he stooped and picked them up and set them on the rack of the piano. Then he sat down and looked her straight in the eyes.

"I'm doing what you told me to do," he said. "I am marrying June Blaine."

She heard and did not hear. Instead there was the rush of a sudden downpour of wind-driven rain. It beat

182

against the French windows, it thundered upon the stones of the terrace. She lifted her head and listened to the sound of the storm.

"We'll not get away tomorrow," she murmured.

He stared at her. "Are you all right, Edith?"

When she did not reply he went to her and took her face between his palms. "I asked you, are you all right, Edith?"

She looked into his eyes. "Yes," she said distinctly.

He released her then but he stood looking down at her. "You've been too long alone, that's what's wrong."

She pushed him away gently. "Oh, no, I'm quite happy being alone. I've learned how."

"I'm still in love with you," he said with bitterness.

"Don't say it!" she cried.

"But I will say it," he insisted. "It's hopeless, I know—but true, for all that!"

"It's not fair to June," she said.

"She knows," he said doggedly. "I couldn't marry her otherwise. Between you and me, I've told her, everything must be the same—forever."

He turned away from her and walked to the window and stared out into the storm. "I hope I'm not trying to substitute her for you!"

This was no longer to be borne. She determined not to bear it. By force she would break the mood, too tense, too charged with emotion.

"Impossible," she declared. "We are two entirely different women!"

In her heart she added, "She has her place—but I have mine!"

But she did not speak the words aloud.

. . . The change in mood continued. Henry entered at this moment to announce luncheon and over the

183

business of food and drink, Jared's appetite excellent, she made a show of mild interest in his plans.

"Shall you marry soon, Jared?"

"After she graduates from college in June."

"Still so young! Lucky you!"

"I've known her for a couple of years, remember!"

"She's a sensible little thing."

"I wouldn't marry her otherwise. I've made it clear to her that I have my work to do and that comes first—always will. It's the penalty for marrying a dedicated scientist."

"Shall you stay at this rehabilitation work?"

"No. Not really. I see now that it's a side job, an avocation. I'll always work at it occasionally. But it's not my real job."

He frowned and she waited. He began again. "I don't know what my work is. Mending broken bodies—yes, of course, but that's not it. Something in mathematics. I love the order, the elegance of mathematics. But even that is merely a tool, a means. I want to discover—"

"What?" She pressed him when he paused.

He lifted eyes half apologetic. "You'll laugh—but it's the only word that fits. I want to discover—the universe."

"Thank God!" she cried softly under her breath.

He frowned again. "Why do you thank God?"

"Because you belong in your laboratory, Jared."

She spoke with such decision that he put down knife and fork.

"How did you know?" he demanded.

"I know you," she said. "I know you are basically an artist and an artist is always seeking revelation. You're not just a technician. You're a creator."

Their eyes met, now unwavering, his in awe, hers in confidence.

"You know!" he whispered.

"Of course," she said quietly. "And so I love you."

. . . It was summer again. She was in a little church, waiting among a few strangers for the wedding march to begin. It was Jared's wedding day. She had gone home in March, the snows of the winter melting except on the mountains. He had not stayed long, a day and a night, but she was not lonely when he left. She knew her place now in his life and her duty to love him as only she could do. She understood that the more she fulfilled her own life, the more wisdom she could learn, the more she could achieve in herself, the more complete she became—yes, even the more perfect, the better her love could serve him. She must be forever the abiding goddess. And this could only be fulfilled if she found her own way to that fulfillment, apart from Jared. But what was the way? Now that she had years ahead, how spend them toward fulfillment? She was her father's daughter in mind and spirit, though her mother had created her flesh. She must, once this wedding was over, go apart and live with herself alone.

There had been no time until now, not really any time: Arnold's death; Edwin, his love and death; Jared and his love and hers, only in its beginning now that its path lay clearly before her. There had been no time. Now there was time, infinite time, until the very end of her life. She need not hurry herself. Now she knew that she, too, must search, quietly and firmly, for her own completion, for were she not complete, she could not take her place in Jared's completion.

The organist was beginning to play the introductory music to marriage, tender music, the mood reverent and subdued. About her the people waited, their faces half smiling as they remembered, each his own remembering. The church was old-fashioned, very simple, almost a country church. Here June had been christened and by the very minister, then young, who was to perform

185

the ceremony. He came in now, wearing his robes. In front of him walked two small boys, choristers, who carried lighted torches. When they reached the altar the small boys lit the candles on either side, and then took their places. The tender music drew to a close. A door to the side of the chancel opened and Jared came in with his best man, someone she did not know, a fellow scientist, he had told her, a brilliant boy of a man, he had said, working in space science. "He lives and breathes on a new level of existence," Jared had said. "He makes the rest of us look earthbound and old hat."

She remembered these words, but her eyes were on Jared. He looked abstracted, far away, almost unconcerned. How well she knew that look, how often her mother had complained of her father.

"Raymond! Do you hear a word I'm saying?"

Sometimes, half laughing, her mother said to those about her, "I don't believe he even heard our marriage ceremony!"

Ah, June must learn to understand this divine abstraction, this cosmic absence! Once, she herself had inquired of a young wife whose young husband had traveled into space.

"Did he come back the same?"

"Not the same," the young wife had said sadly. "Never quite the same."

Ah, but June must be proud, not sad! And then, as though at the thought of June, the wedding march broke joyfully across the air. The audience rose and turned to watch the pretty procession, a little girl in a short pink frock walked down the aisle, scattering rose petals, behind her a tiny boy carrying a white satin ring cushion, and then, one after the other, three bridesmaids—young, all so young, all pretty in pink frocks. And at last June in bride's white, the gleam of satin, the froth of lace, she walking beside her father, her white-gloved hand in his elbow, a tall graying man, still handsome, a famous man in the world, a great man in his way. But none would be greater than Jared. This was her lifework.

Then almost immediately it was over, the ceremony stripped to its essentials.

"I don't want any nonsense," Jared had said firmly.

There was no nonsense. The brief vows were said, he came down the aisle, head held high, and June clung to his arm, smiling bravely. A dart of compassion struck her heart. This young wife! It would not be easy to be Jared's wife. She must think, too, of June, for June unhappy would be a burden Jared must not bear. And yet, she told herself, she must never interfere.

She laughed inside herself. Only a goddess could fulfill all that she was demanding of herself. This, then, was her first task, to make of herself a goddess, the first task and the most difficult. She must set herself apart if she was to fulfill the monumental task, which in itself must be perfection.

Someone, a young man, an usher, came to escort her down the aisle, and she walked to the door and out of the church to her waiting car. An hour's solitary drive, and she was not lonely, an hour's solitary drive and she was at the house again, and only when she entered the door did she remember there was a reception somewhere, at June's home somewhere, a wedding cake to be cut, all of which she had forgotten, as abstracted in her own way as Jared in his, but she had her own dreams. Not to be fulfilled in this house, nor in any other in which she had ever lived! The knowledge came with the suddenness of conviction. She must build herself a house of her own, in the place which she had chosen so blindly, a place by the sea. The plans were where she had put them in a drawer in her desk. She had put them there months ago, not knowing whether she would ever finish them. Now she knew.

She took off her hat and tossed it to a chair. She

went to the library, to her desk, and opened the drawer. The plans were there, as she had left them. She sat down and studied them. She could see the house as though it were already standing solitary on the cliff, overlooking the sea. The idea in itself was reality. As Edwin had said, the very idea of immortality made reality. Now the idea of the house, of herself, of Jared, were realities.

She heard a cough at the door. She looked up and saw Weston waiting.

"If you please, madame," he said, "is there anyone here for dinner?"

"Only I—myself," she said.

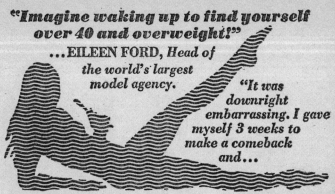